McDonell, Terry
   California bloodstock.

CALIFORNIA BLOODSTOCK

CALIFORNIA

One of those life and death, love and infinity
sagas set in the mountains and on the
beaches of the Pacific . . . with horses

BLOODSTOCK

TERRY McDONELL

Macmillan Publishing Co., Inc.

NEW YORK

Macmillan Publishing Co., Inc.
866 Third Avenue, New York, N.Y. 10022
Collier Macmillan Canada, Ltd.

Library of Congress Cataloging in Publication Data

McDonell, Terry.
  California bloodstock.

  I. Title.
PZ4.M134895Cal   [PS3563.A29143]   813'.5'4
ISBN 0-02-583150-X   79-25725

First Printing 1980

Printed in the United States of America

*For my mother,
who as far as I know
invented artichokes*

California is somewhere else.

Joan Didion,
Notes from a Native Daughter

CALIFORNIA BLOODSTOCK

PROLOGUE

1/Taya

Taya wasn't a Californiana but it didn't matter anymore. Especially now.

She climbed up into the dunes, picking her way through the pampas grass. West, off toward the palisades, she could make out a grizzly and two cubs feeding on a whale carcass that had drifted onto the beach. She looked back out over the flats and saw a pack of dogs sloshing through the shallows spooking the herons and loons. The wind gusted, fanning her hair off her back. California, she suddenly sensed, was going to swallow itself. The Worm Eaters have had it. And the Animal People too, probably. What dark thoughts for such a beautiful girl.

Of course none of this was California's fault. It must have started out there somewhere between the

Rocky Mountains and the Sierra Nevada when Buckdown and Slant made the deal and wound up sleeping with the same woman. At least that's where it
started for Taya. She knew that now.

ONE

2/Buckdown

Buckdown hated animals, all of them. Said he wanted to kill them all. Confronted by such a colossal lack of *mana*, the primitives he dealt with could not draw the line where their shock stopped and their fear began. And coupled with the fact that Buckdown had imaginatively developed his own profane sign language, this managed to hold him in a powerful light, especially among the purveyors of big dreams. Indeed, he was perceived as one of the only big guns on the pelt scene to offer interesting potential as an ally as well as an enemy. Thus one Big Bowl, a high-rolling Western Shoshone, was considered shrewd when he determined to marry one of his many daughters to the mountain man to insure certain trade arrangements. The year was 1830.

Buckdown had been wondering if marriage might

head off what had been sneaking up on him lately: his own wretched life. It was his little secret of course, but the simple pleasures of riding, stalking, shooting (blood slurping?) had gone flat on him. It had come upon him slowly over his years under the big sky, but now as surely as the sun rose every morning, each sunset sucked him deeper into the indifferent vacuum of a lonely man. He had become bored with scenery. At dusk in some empty basin or on some solitary ridge he would go about the business of feeding himself and then sit cross-legged through the twilight and into the darkness until suddenly it was dawn and he had not slept a wink. So sure enough, when Big Bowl suggested a wedding, the idea hit Buckdown with the precision of a rifle hammer locking into place behind a powder cap. That is, with a click. Certainly he was not the first to marry out of something other than love. Plus, he needed something to do at night.

Buckdown stood tranced throughout the ceremony and pleased his new in-laws enormously with a posture that at least appeared to be resolute while his mind played forward over the possibilities. No one had any idea what perverse jingle-jangles were dancing behind his glazed eyes, and a good time was had by all; even the bride, who danced in place with sexy little shuffle steps.

On through the skindancing and the bone music and the dog-eating, Buckdown stood with his bride. He looked from moment to moment almost shy and bewildered then terrified and crazy and laughing.

Chattering gaggles of adolescents and old-timers as-
saulted the couple with loving pinches and playful
pokes to the genitals, or clicked out proxy advice
from the Animal People. The warriors sat off alone or
in tight little clusters smoking the sweet pipe loads
provided by Big Bowl. The afternoon stretched
out. Which turned out to be just fine with Buckdown.

Maybe his bride's dancing had spooked him.
Maybe he had been alone for too long. Anyway his
gulping doubts had bubbled up. In fact, the loping
fantasies that had so lathered his instincts earlier
gave way to a nervousness that definitely had his
goat by bedtime. And sadly into the night under the
conjugal robes there came nothing past some explor-
atory petting. Too bad, and imagine the mutual chagrin when Buckdown finally, in the sweats of
rationalization, rolled muttering away from his
bride.

I will not mate like an animal, he said.

By morning he could barely look at her, let alone
talk it over. He had lost the power of speech. Nothing to do then but get the hell out; and he took off.
Embarrassed by his mute foolishness she followed
him, never more than a half-mile behind, beseeching
the Animal People in song not to defer her youth.
Ridiculous perhaps, but in this hide-and-seek par-
allax the newlyweds headed west. At least it was
Buckdown's favorite direction.

They rode through bright, windy days into a wilderness so vast and quiet from horizon to horizon
that the sky stretched low enough over the curve of

the earth for Buckdown to reach up and touch it from the saddle. But he never felt like it.

Then suddenly there was Slant, sitting on a rock in the middle of what he was bemoaning as nowhere.

3/Slant

Considering his circumstances, Slant was remarkably well-dressed, sporting as he did a cream-colored antelope suede frontier suit. Such outfits were produced east of the Potomac for gentlemen who wished to affect the look of those who had been west of the Missouri. Never mind that it was filthy, Slant's had obviously been tailored to the highest refinement. You could tell by the details: arrow-darted cuffs, flapped pockets, jodhpur inseam patches, and epaulets. It was a real dandy suit.

In Buckdown's bachelor days, he would no doubt have jumped all over Slant. But as it was, Buckdown was more than a bit distracted by the empty hatch of his honeymoon. And remember that since his first guilty morning as a husband, he had had nothing to say.

What a retard, Slant thought, after running through his sophisticated repertoire of salutations and ice breakers, while Buckdown stared blankly at him with all the charm and effectiveness of a plugged rifle barrel.

Reining up her pony between them with the appropriate introductions, Buckdown's bride looked to Slant like the princess she was. He bowed like a cavalier and became the first and only man ever to call her Mrs. Buckdown.

Noting that something was suddenly up, Buckdown turned, grimly flirtatious, to his wife and told her that it was good to see her again.

Good to hear from you, she whispered back.

4/The Deal

Apparently Slant had been traveling with an expedition of explorers and businessmen as the company's secretary and naturalist, his general responsibility, as he saw it, being to chronicle the opening of the West. Then one day, for reasons that remain obscure, they had confiscated his journals and ditched him. And there he was.

Slant explained the absurdity of it all, insisting that he had been undeservedly fucked over by not one, but count 'um, forty-six of his own countrymen and a nigger. But no matter, now that he had met the Buckdowns. Slant, you see, was a gentleman and a journalist with connections to any number of story papers in the East. What he was looking for, he said, was the literature of history; and boy did he bet that the Buckdowns had some stories between them. And, oh yes, there was good money in good stories.

Buckdown said he knew a few and, aiming to brag his way into his wife's respect, invited Slant to ride along. There was more to it, of course. When he had noticed Slant's interest in her, he had also noticed that the most important thing that was up was between his legs. For her part, Mrs. Buckdown thought Slant just as crazy and interesting as her husband had seemed when he first came loping into her father's salt camp.

As it turned out, the three of them entered into an agreement of sorts and began collaborating on various levels. There was the literature of history which, on the surface at least, had gotten the ball rolling; there was the communality of rough travel through a landscape all but overrun by beasts and birds that also appeared to be heading west; and there was sex.

It seems that Buckdown was turned on by his wife turning on Slant, which was so easy she didn't have to try, which, in turn, sort of turned her on. And from there it was just an easy sashay into the wanton metaphysics of the big easy question: Why not?

They started diddling like minks, not that there was anything tacky about it. No, even that first night it was all relatively soft and refined, not to mention good for mental health. And out where they were there was precedent, if you believed the Animal People.

5/The Wilderness Family

Strange, so strange the dymanics of sin and the doings of sinners. Soon Slant and Buckdown were spending hours in front of the fireplace in a dugout cabin high in the mountains, the former asking rude questions and taking notes, the latter mostly bragging. Meanwhile, the little woman, as Slant had taken to calling her, went about the wood gathering, rabbit snaring, and various other chores necessary to keep the three of them alive through the winter.

When she thought about it, she became somewhat befuddled by the structure of her married life, but she certainly wasn't bitter. Her father, she would tell herself, had more than one wife at a time; and, as he had once told her, the daughters of eagles are eagles too. Besides, she aimed to please and enjoyed doing it with the two of them taking turns (always Slant first) in the furry darkness.

She pulled the pattern of their days and nights together around her body like a robe, and when she began laughing in the mornings they became like a family. She would tease, and both Buckdown and Slant would act like grateful children, making up secrets to tell her and showing off.

That's the way it went with the three of them high on the eastern slope of the Sierra Nevada from the fall of 1830 to the spring of 1831. It seemed natural enough.

When the snow began to melt and slide into the rivers, the manuscript was close to complete in rough draft and she was eight-months pregnant. The growing family felt content and prosperous. Buckdown insisted on taking over the wood gathering. Slant joked that even the beasts wandering around them in the wilderness were pleased with the weight of what had been accomplished. She laughed and agreed.

At night, their even breathing drifted through the trees, and they dreamed together of a ferocious wolf with knives in his mouth who kept an eye on the surrounding woods for them.

Days, while the wolf slept, found them almost giddy with pride, bouncing happily through the chores which they had come to view as favors for each other. Most afternoons they made long walks up and down the swollen gorges, making plans.

Buckdown had spent years in the wilds without noticing the smell of sage or the soft lavender shading that explosions of lupin threw along the skirts of granite cliffs. It was as if he had suddenly tripped over the concept of spring.

Slant was naturally a bit more sophisticated about it. He observed all manner of furry little creatures darting out into the fresh season and was reminded of obscure and pornographic Persian poetry.

Walking brightly between them, she guessed that she was the first woman, certainly the first Shoshone woman, to live on the sunny side of what Slant called a *ménage à trois*. She picked out a name and hoped for a daughter.

6/Spring Wolf

When she died in childbirth the two men felt a shock as instant and infuriating as they had not known since their own birth days. Slant turned surly and morose. Buckdown fell wildly into despair. They argued over who had loved her more and accused each other of not paying attention. So preoccupied were they with where to fix the blame that the child, a tiny girl baby with shiny eyes and pale freckles across her cheekbones, almost died on them.

After much bitter conjecture about specific responsibilities and the meaning of life in general, the two men could no longer stand the sight of each other. Both considered murder. Finally one morning after discovering the decaying carcass of a large wolf less than a hundred yards below the cabin, Buckdown went wandering alone out along the traplines he had ignored for so many months. Slant went south with both the manuscript and the child. They thought they were through with each other, finished. But destinies have a way of mingling, especially when beautiful children are involved, and they were to meet again on the cusp of another life.

Significant in the ultimate turn of events was the publication, in 1835 by Harper & Bros., of *The Frontier Adventures of Francis Buckdown: As Written from His Own Dictation by T. D. Slant, Esq.* The book received mixed reviews and sold poorly in New York. It did better along the frontier and later in Europe, although it was difficult to find. It cost a nickel.

TWO

7/Monterey

Her mother had planned to call her Melting-Snow-
of-Winter-That-Chases-Despair, but it had not
worked out. Old T. D. Slant and everybody else
around Monterey in 1846 called her Taya. Only Slant
knew why. She was a quick, breezy child with rich
black hair and eyes that reminded Slant of wet grey
stones. And there was a bounce to her, a rhythm in
her small tight body that made men notice her. She
was fifteen and had been noticing them back for
some time.

She passed the customhouse with its Mexican flag
snapping in the morning wind and trotted her big
gelding across the sandy street, heading up the hill
to a place where she could see far out over the Pacific.
She liked to sit in a certain little grove of cypress and
watch the whales spouting playfully south. When

there were no whales she would watch the wide blue flatness for ships. But most of all, she liked to be alone and think about bodies, her body and how other bodies might fit with it. She fell back in the dune grass and swung her feet toward the grey clouds forming over the bay. She turned her ankles in small circles and moved her hands slowly over her small breasts. Fine. She was fine if anyone wanted to know.

If she had felt like it she could have turned back down the hill and maybe caught a glimpse of old T. D. leaving the office for his morning drink. Instead she rode down to the beach to dig clams.

When she climbed to the top of the hill again it was late in the afternoon. Still no whales, but looking down into town she saw three men ride up in front of where she lived. They seemed to argue over something, pointing at the sign over the door that old T. D. was so proud of. She didn't recognize them but could see that they were dressed like Americans, mostly in skins. She wondered how old they were.

Most of the Americans showing up in Monterey lately were a lot more pleased with old T. D.'s sign and what it told the Mexicans and Californios than they were with old T. D. himself. The sign said that there was an American newspaper in California.

Old T. D. Slant was the founder, editor, and publisher of the *California American* and had been since he showed up and bought the only printing press in the territory from Vallejo back in 1838 when the Russians were still making everybody nervous. His readers generally believed what they read but they sure as hell didn't trust Slant personally. The principle of *it takes one to know one* explains why. After all, Slant had wandered west with the rest of them, and they knew who they were. So Slant was said to cheat brilliantly at monte, to have shot three men from ambush, and to be looking for a free lunch. He claimed to be the same age as the century but was lying by twenty years. He was especially vain about the curly auburn beard which he kept as sweetly perfumed as a French whore's twat. Or so he said.

Why Taya lived with him was a minor local mystery. He told folks that she was his mistress, his child, or both, depending on how he felt like playing it at the time. He was considered shrewd and eccentric.

If anyone wanted to know what had brought him to California, he would snort smugly into his sweet-smelling whiskers and start whispering like a conspirator about spreading civilization. There were some, however, who claimed that on one especially tropical night on the plaza, when he had been lushing up large quantities of mission wine with Freemont's topographical engineers, he had suddenly blurted out something a good deal closer to the truth.

I came to California to retire and fuck around, he had shouted.

And in this he was not alone.

8/Sewey and the Burgetts

Even for 1846 the men that Taya saw from the hill were a trinity of bad examples. Galon Burgett, his brother Millard, and Josiah Sewey were three old scoundrels who had been knocking around west of the Missouri River since they deserted together from the War of 1812.

Galon was small but well formed, smart as a weasel and rather handsome. Woman usually liked him until they got to know him. His younger brother Millard was smaller yet, barely over five feet tall, and simpleminded. Colicky tufts of white hair sprouted from his empty skull just above each ear, making him appear even dumber than he was, which was difficult. Once, when they were kids, one of their ma's cousins made a joke about Millard and the whole family sleeping together in the same bed and their pa had shot the cousin in the foot. Galon and Millard held hands and giggled while the cousin bled to death. They grew up close. Another time, years later, Galon had used his skinning knife to make a Santa Fe whore give Millard a tongue bath.

Their pal Josiah Sewey had wolf eyes and big scarred hands. He looked like the strong, mean old man that he was. He made a real good bully when he felt like it, which was often. There were even times when he felt like shoving Galon around a little, but for one reason or another he never did. Once, Sewey shot one of his own fingers off by accident and was embarrassed about it until Galon made up a story for him to tell. The story went that Sewey had shot it off on purpose, on a bet. Sewey thought the story was perfect and loved to tell it. He liked to hang around with Galon because he admired his mind.

Galon was the idea man, the leader. He pulled a grimy wolfskin pouch from his saddle and led Millard and Sewey into the office of California's American newspaper. It was the same year that Alexander Cartwright designed the first official baseball diamond and the very same day that the Knickerbocker Club in New York held its first bowling tournament. East is east and west is west, as old T. D. Slant was fond of suggesting at the time. Even the sports were different.

9/Slander

You ever hear of Galon Burgett?

It was a real sly question coming as it did from Galon himself. Slant wasn't sure. He snorted ostentatiously into his beard and searched his memory. Yes, he had heard of a Galon Burgett but he couldn't ferret out just where or how.

We come about the book, Galon told him.

A pack of lies, hissed Sewey.

Before Slant could respond, Galon had the evidence out of the pouch. With a flourish, he tossed it on the desk in front of Slant. The coverless, chewed-up volume fell obediently open to the passage Galon wanted. Something about cowardly and unscrupulous dealings with the Shoshone, and a general pettifogging dishonesty on the part of the two varlet brothers named Burgett. The passage went for three pages without a break, ending finally with an explanation of how one Francis Buckdown had been forced on numerous occasions to publicly box the Burgetts' riffraff ears.

Slant noticed that someone, probably Galon Burgett, had been engaging the book in cryptic debates.
The words *bullshit* and *goddamn lie* were scrawled
here and there in the margins with such bold strokes
that the blotches of dried animal blood and other grit
that covered the pages passed here and there for
punctuation.

Slant was not happy. Tentatively he allowed that
he recognized the book as one that he might have
had something to do with.

I wouldn't be bragging, Galon told him.

Sewey snarled like a dog.

Millard started to pant.

Blow it the other way. Slant popped the book shut
and insisted that it wasn't his work in any true literary sense. Any fool could see that.

Oh yeah, Galon argued. Then what about Hippolyte Weed who had given him the book and who was
also plenty pissed off on account of certain lies about
him? And what about the picture of Indian fighting
that was supposed to be on the cover that Weed had
traded to Counsel for some rope? Wasn't Slant's
name on it? And what about a lot of other things?

Slant chortled self-consciously. So maybe they had
never seen the cover. Slant hoped not. That might
explain the misunderstanding.

It was getting sticky. Sewey had pulled a nasty-
looking knife out of his boot and was waving it in
the air, demanding that Slant get to the parts about
him. And indeed, there were several passages in the
book suggesting dark venalities on the part of a certain ticket-of-leave cur named Sewey. Slant finessed
Sewey and his knife with an adroit snort and pulled

a crisp new copy of the book from the shelf behind him. Galon grabbed it.

The cover depicted a large man, sporting much fringe, in the act of dispatching a pack of obviously wild but rather puny savages. Their dead bodies heaped around him as they fell under his tomahawk and noble purpose. It was Buckdown all right. The Burgetts and Sewey studied the cover, fascinated. It was him for sure but he never. . .

Slant concentrated on Galon, pointing to a line of small type under the title.

See here, he said. See here where it says *As Written from His Own Dictation by T.D. Slant, Esq.* That means that I simply wrote down what Buckdown told me. What he told me to write down.

Galon was not impressed. He insisted that Slant still wrote it.

But not in the pure literary sense, Slant argued.

Thus they were discussing literary sense when Taya walked in with a sack of clams.

10/La Cantina del Futuro Proximo

What a disappointment. Taya's smile dropped to a low curve of disdain as she sized them up. Three smelly old farts. Not at all what she had in mind.

Shy, Slant explained as Taya walked past them without a word and disappeared out the door to the patio. Sewey and the Burgetts stared after her, grunting to each other, sizing her up. Young blood?

Some kind of breed, from Sewey.

Crow or Shoshone, from Galon.

Pretty, from Millard.

Yes, said Slant, herding them toward the front door, my mistress and not the local worm-eating variety. A princess, in fact, among her own people and developing into a real fine civilized lady here under my wing, shall we say. But to the business at hand. Shall we adjourn to a more appropriate setting?

Millard thought this meant that they would all go out in the street and have a gunfight, but Slant led them instead to his local cantina.

La Cantina del Futuro Proximo was the most popular cantina in Monterey and was thus usually crowded with mental-health problems. Sewey and the Burgetts felt right at home. Slant sat them down at a corner table and went to the bar for a bottle of brandy. At the next table, four men and an old woman were playing monte, a game similar to blackjack but easier to cheat at. Millard was captivated. The old woman noticed and winked at him. He didn't understand.

What's that they're playing? Millard whispered to Galon.

Never mind, we got business.

You can handle it, Galon.

Millard, Galon scolded, is that all you care about them lies? You crackbrain!

Millard hung his head. He was ashamed. He tried to make it up to Galon by squinting as mean as he could at Slant, who was returning to the table with a bottle and four small glasses. But Slant just smiled and dealt out the glasses.

Over the first two drinks, Slant conceded that, yes,

the boys might have a legitimate grievance. With Buckdown, however, not with him.

Well, Galon said, we just want it fixed.

We want all them books fixed, Sewey added.

Over the third and fourth drinks, Slant explained the difficulties. Harper & Brothers back in New York couldn't possibly track down and call back all the copies, even if they could be convinced of such an obligation, which, given the nature of the publishing business, was unlikely at best.

Balls, Sewey grumbled and started fingering the knife in his boot.

I wouldn't be bragging, said Millard.

Galon coughed but didn't speak. He watched Slant like a cat toying with a flower, considering the possibilities.

Over the fifth and sixth drinks, Slant insisted that their argument was with Buckdown. After all, it was Buckdown who had initiated the misunderstanding in the first place. Any and all gnawing bones should be picked with him.

Look here, Slant, Galon said softly, we don't give a shit about any Harper or how many brothers he's got and we'll take care of Buckdown after we fix the literature side of it. I've got it all figured out and you don't even have to pay us.

Yeah, Sewey said, sticking his knife in the table for emphasis, Counsel says that asshole probably got rich off them lies.

Over the seventh and eighth drinks, Slant launched a buoyant explanation of the economics of publishing. Nobody makes any money, etc. . . .

Balls, Sewey growled, now fondling his knife.

Galon was more reasonable. All you got to do, he told Slant, is write a book about us.

About you three?

Slant's mind churned. A moon-brain scam eclipsed his reason. He reached slowly for the bottle, and over the ninth and tenth drinks outlined the amount of time and effort such a book would require and then, after an appropriate pause, snuck in the necessity of a small advance.

Forget it!

It was determined that Galon, Millard, and Sewey would give Slant a quick outline of the basic truth and he could fill in around the edges while they saw to other business. Galon had it all worked out.

Yeah, said Millard, inspired into his first complete sentence of the day, while we're gone you can fill in around the edges with literature.

Right. And the bottle was empty.

Back on the patio, Taya sat in the shade shelling clams. She wondered if old T. D. was lying about sleeping with her again. Probably. She wondered if anyone ever believed him. She ate a raw clam. It died going down.

11/California Patio

The boys had never been to a bar-b-que before. All they knew was that they were always eating outside anyway and didn't think it was so hot, especially when they were in civilization. But when Slant explained it as a local custom, they figured what the hell and wound up sitting out on the patio.

The tan ground was raked smooth with clean little rake lines all running in one orderly direction. Pale geraniums, soft magenta and dusty pink, flushed along the whitewashed adobe walls. A spreading cypress, with fading blue and white lupin peeking from its roots, shaded a redwood table set with earthen pots and milky brown platters. The light was soft, dying peacefully, stretching shadows east toward smooth hills bathed in lavender by the sunset. But all was not monotonous pastel. Here and there bright yellow and orange poppies broke loudly through the quiet palette like the weeds they are.

Galon coughed into the stillness. Then again and again, unleashing a jangling chain of spasms from deep in his chest. His noisy fit sent a family of swallows winging from their nest in the cypress. They fluttered in alarmed circles over the patio.

It must be the air, Sewey laughed, too much grease in the air. Galon bent from the waist and rode himself out with a series of convulsive spits at the ground.

The swallows settled back on their branches, but not for long. Millard, who had been carving his initials in the base of the cypress, felt so bad about his brother's cough that he started chucking pieces of bark at the nervous birds.

Slant was inside talking to Taya, telling her to stay out of sight. Naturally, she wanted to know why. Because, Slant explained with an unsteady intensity, the three men on the patio were rather upset with

her father and himself. Something about the literature of history. And they were also looking for a free
lunch.

Father? Taya was totally unprepared. Not that she
wasn't interested. She would often stare into mir-
rors, dissecting her reflection, noting that yes, she
might be the daughter of an Indian princess like old
T. D. said, with his talk of how he had traded for her
because she was such a beautiful baby. But she never
got the story the same twice and besides, who ever
heard of a Worm Eater with freckles.

Yet she had these feelings, and knew moments,
languishing in the half sleep of rainy mornings,
when she saw herself on a brave and sensual journey, scouring all manner of terrain, searching out the
gene pools and nostalgic tumors of closeted family
secrets that would account for her smoky intuitions.
She wanted to know if history repeated itself beyond
shanks of bone and hanks of hair, but she had never
had a clue. Until now.

Old T. D. left her to join the three old farts on the
patio. She leaned against the wall in the darkening
pantry, sensing the past and the future at the same
time. It was traumatic, intoxicating. Father? She
hadn't even read the book.

12/The Big Spit

The swallows were still circling when Slant returned
to the patio and went to work tossing steaks around
on a grilled fire pit. Millard and Sewey were pleased,

but Galon kept coughing and spitting into the fire. He ignored the food except to pick now and then at a plate of tiny figs intended as dessert while Millard and Sewey gnawed at the meat like wolverines and gulped handfuls of fried clams rolled in tortillas. Once they had stuffed themselves, it was on to more brandy and the literary business at hand, with Taya listening from the pantry.

The conversation was difficult to follow, but about this Buckdown . . . this transgressing double-dealing viper turd . . . this venal captain of falsehoods . . . this polluted forger of truth . . . this dirty rat . . . this liar. He should be made to grovel in the pornographic bile of his own sucking counterfeits. Cysts, sties, carbuncles, cavities, slivers, and ingrown horns should come to him as only a partial reward for his salacious frauds. He should be lashed, rib-roasted, larruped, pummeled, stomped, drawn and quartered, and creamed. Something to that effect.

Galon seemed to be feeling better. He led Millard and Sewey into a righteous frenzy about how they were going to serve that son-of-a-buck Buckdown right. Slant nodded and made cosmetic notes while the tremors of drunkenness rattling up from the patio chased off the swallows for good. Suddenly, Galon lurched to his feet.

The big spit, he announced, and staggered off.

Slant grabbed the pause in the conversation and excused himself to the pantry for another bottle and his small silver-plated belly gun just in case.

Inside he found Taya loading the gun. Her eyes flashed wet and cold at him, like bullets in a shot

glass. He asked her for the gun. She shook her head.
You're drunk, she said.

Indeed he was, drunk enough to forget himself
and blunder through an explanation of how he was
just faking it with the Burgetts and Sewey, and how
he had no intention of writing down any of their
swill.

Don't you see, he said, gesturing for the gun, I'm
just putting them on.

A big mistake and too bad. Framed in the small
open window behind them was Galon Burgett, his
mouth smeared with vomit, a whip cracking in his
bloodshot eyes.

13/Southern Style

The rape of Melting-Snow-of-Winter-That-Chases-
Despair and the castration of Theodosius D'Arta-
gnon Slant took the boys about ten minutes. They
accomplished it in what Sewey referred to as southern style. Semi-southern style is closer to the truth,
however, since both victims were not conscious
throughout, and the idea was always to make each
watch what happened to the other. Just ask any
Oakie.

While Galon held Taya, Millard and Sewey gagged
old T. D. and hung him by his wrists from the main
redwood ceiling beam. He kicked frantically for a
moment, running hopelessly in the still air, getting
nowhere. Sewey spun him like a field-dressed animal, and he went limp at the end of the twisting rope

as they bent Taya back like a sapling over the desk. Then an almost isometric quiet, broken only by the sound of fabric being torn from her breasts and crotch. Finally, her one and only scream.

As Sewey and the Burgetts took their turns, Taya strained as if against drowning, counting their thrusts as days, then months. Old T. D. clenched his eyes against the sight of her finely grained skin glistening under their sweat until he sensed that she had passed out, and he looked with hopeless resignation to see them turning their attention to him.

Sewey said he'd handle it, and he did. Drop his pants for him, he told Millard, and when that was done Sewey grabbed old T. D. by the balls and made a quick swipe with his knife. The scrotum sack and its vein-laced contents came away in his fist.

When she came to, Taya was alone with old T. D., whom the boys had left dangling in shock and bleeding to death over a puddle of blood. She cut him down quickly and, without thinking, began to treat him like a gelded colt. First she tied off the spermatic artery then cleaned him out and packed him with pledgets of tow that she dipped in a bottle of tincture of muriate of iron. Either he would heal by adhesion or he wouldn't. As she rubbed him dry she wasn't so sure about herself.

THREE

14/Taya

When she could walk again, Taya made her way to
one of the deep pools above the crumbling Mission
San Carlos Borromeo on the Carmel River. Easing in
and out of the still water, she carefully examined
herself. Over and over, her delicate hands stroked
down her body, coming together ultimately like two
streams at the mouth of her own mysterious ocean.

She knew what had happened. When she was
twelve, she had seen Mexican soldiers take the wife
and daughter of a renegade Worm Eater behind the
horse barn next to the customhouse. And she knew
what happened next. The word would go around and
she would be expected to put out for every horned
freebooter who staggered through with a hard-on.

Thus a dense garden of vengeful plants began to
grow in her mind, and when it reached the propor-

tions of a forest, she walked to the beach, using the timber to build herself a fort, a storeroom really, for the twisting and urgent tortures she began designing for Sewey and the Burgetts. As the sun faded behind the ocean she stepped back from what she had built and heard wind rushing through the beams.

The rent was due.

15/Hasta la Vista

It warmed every rattlesnake heart in California that nobody ever stayed in cahoots with anybody else for very long. Maybe it had something to do with the land itself. What with opportunities crystallizing every morning like dew hardening into candy on the bright petals of lilies, fireweed, and pussy-paws. Who knew what tempting chances would show up like specials on the daily menu, along with the glazed oranges carmelized in wheat porridge and the sweet and sour calf hearts soaking in *chilimato salsa*. Even three old pals like Sewey and the Burgetts didn't stay together long once they digested the possibilities.

They had ridden out of Monterey in the dark. At dawn they were passing out of the Carmel Valley, headed for the Salinas River. By noon, the sun was blasting at the dry brush and they heard insects clicking like bones in the sandy dust. Galon's lungs felt like sacks of hot dirt and he coughed over and over in the brittle air. Suddenly, he pulled up and dry-puked from the saddle.

Millard wondered if Galon was feeling bad. He was always concerned about his brother. Sewey thought it was funny.

Yeah, Galon, he goaded, you feeling okay? You been doing that with some regularity lately, I've noticed.

Fuck you, Galon shouted, gagging again with the effort. Fuck both of you! Who needs you!

When Galon composed himself, they rode on in anxious silence, all three brooding over what Galon had said.

They stopped for supper at the Mission San Juan Bautista and demanded to eat inside. Galon had some broth and closed his eyes. Millard and Sewey gobbled up a rabbit fricassee and some lime chicken while a fat old padre bemoaned the shortage of Worm Eaters to tend to the work of the mother-shepherd church. Out the window, Sewey counted more than thirty scabby Worm Eaters scratching in the dark with crude hoes. A fat untended ox dragged a splintering wooden cart with a broken axle aimlessly among them. Sewey found the scene inspiring.

The next morning he rode off alone with only a loose agreement to meet up with the Burgetts at some later date. He seemed in a great hurry.

See you around, is all he said.

Or in hell, Galon shouted after him and told Millard they would ride west, toward Santa Cruz.

They found it growing up around a defunct mission and took up immediately with a fraternity of grubby southerners who hung around a distillery run by Kentucky-born Isaac Grahm. Grahm was highly respected. He had been plotting and schem-

ing in California for a number of years and had done
well, if you forget the various efforts by numerous
Californios to have him deported as a dangerous for-
eigner. He and the Burgetts hit it off at once and they
were his guests for more than a week, drinking raw
whisky and bullshitting.

Galon was quick-minded as a drop latch but having only just arrived in California his understanding
of its politics was, as he put it, as fuzzy as a mad
cat's back. He wondered if there was any law
around.

Naw, Grahm assured him, anybody with any balls
just makes up his own.

Galon was relieved. It wasn't that he was especially concerned about their fun with the girl, but he
had been feeling vaguely anxious whenever he
thought about what Sewey had done to Slant.

Well, fuck him if he can't take a joke, Grahm
roared when Galon told him the story. Ha, ha, ha.

So when the Burgetts rode on, Galon was chuck-
ling to himself at how easily such things could be
made into jokes. Which goes to show how right he
sometimes was for all the wrong reasons.

16/Slant

Slant lost most of his illusions along with his balls.
He knew without thinking that it would be useless
to report the incident to the greaser authorities. He
didn't have any confidence in American justice

either, but he did file a formal complaint with Thomas Larkin, the American consul, probably just to test the density of his new status. What would Larkin say?

Larkin was a big-eared, plodding, dry-goods-oriented transplant from Massachusetts who dealt primarily in skins, soap, and manifest destiny. He wore black linen suits and was known from Mazatlan to Mystic as a man who definitely knew how to fry more than one fish at a time. He had bartered his way into Californio society, and since about 1840 had been carrying on like some kind of one-man chamber of commerce and tourist bureau, writing letters full of hard-sell descriptions of California as paradise to the New York papers. Larkin called for pioneers the way that most men ask their wives to pass the salt, and quietly supplied any warships, whalers, or trading vessels touching his coast without regard for their affiliations.

He propped his black boots up on his shiny mahogany desk and leaned back grinning at Slant. So they cut your balls off.

Just what Slant was afraid of, snide ridicule. Larkin rocked in his chair and chuckled that if Slant could round up the culprits he would be glad to officiate at a trial.

Big deal, Slant shouted, limping toward the door.

You never know, Larkin called after him. Hang in there.

Very funny. Slant's paranoia conjured hideous jokes being circulated at his expense. He imagined former friends and business associates yucking it up over his condition as they sat around drinking and gambling at the Cantina del Futuro Proximo. Sticks and stones . . . indeed. He dropped from sight.

Days, he convalesced in bed, cursing out of control at the vacancy between his legs. Nights, he brooded on the patio. And the deeper he brooded, the icier the winds he felt blowing up his thighs. He felt his manly juices deserting him, dripping away. He decided to get out of town, to flee. If he couldn't have a miracle in his sad old life, he could at least be left alone. But where?

Finally, after considering a return east, he determined to point his future north, toward Yerba Buena, a small settlement at the head of San Francisco Bay noted for keeping secrets and not giving a shit who showed up. A good place to forget about everything.

Ironically, it was on the very night he made his decision that his past fell in on him like a crumbling library. The keystone had moved.

FOUR

17/New York

T.D. Slant wooed Miss Pippa Lippencot on the muddy sidewalks of New York in the spring of 1825. An interesting year, 1825, and not just for Slant.

Buckdown helped organize a trappers' rendezvous which drew a large and rowdy congress of Indians, mountain men, and eastern fur dealers to the baking flats of the Great Salt Lake. The affair turned into a six-week drinking and gambling toot during which more than $100,000 worth of furs changed hands.

And further west in California, the first duly appointed Mexican governor proposed importing six hundred apes from Guatemala, dressing them as soldiers, and turning them loose to confound the American mountain men his spies told him would soon be heading his way from the Great Salt Lake with their heads full of avarice and their souls full of animal murder. All of them on the make, just like Slant.

Slant was forty-five years old at the time, and a lettered liar. After a cruise through the *Citizens Advertising and Social Directory* and several afternoons studying the *Commissioners' Folio of Real Estate Maps,* Slant set his cap at Pippa Lippencot and went to work. Pippa was tall and pale, thick-haired but rather stark-looking in the manner of women who never expect to have any fun. She was also the vainest thirty-year-old spinster on Fifth Avenue, and took pleasure in what she felt as a rather eclectic superiority. They were made for each other like pearls and swine.

You ride like an Indian princess, he would tell her as they rode up the thicket-lined avenues of a social order she understood to be fixed forever. An Indian princess, yes. She would stiffen in her awkward sidesaddle and admit that, yes, she knew she did.

She had what was known in horse circles as a bad seat. Slant knew this, of course, but he also knew a good deal more. Her father, Backhouse Fish Lippencot, was right up there with Astor, Vanderbilt, and the Brevoorts when it came to money and land—that matched team pulling the shit wagon of power out of the previous century. Old man Lippencot was only a little more conservative than those who went on to be richer than God by the time the Animal People were on the run.

Privately, Pippa was a bit wild. That she drank sherry at the solitary little teas she threw for herself was her little secret. Ditto for the fact that she had lost her virginity to a French expansionist on the continental tour that was all but mandatory for young ladies of her class. But people talk, and when she expressed interest in the new science of phrenology, it was said that she was one of those modern girls. You know, the kind that like to experiment. So she had a reputation. One of Slant's newfound New York cronies told him that when she left for Europe she smelled so sweet that one of them frogs she ran into over there probably popped her cherry with his nose.

Well now. Slant, new in town, broke, and horny for privilege, just in from Florida where he had failed to get rich with a newspaper of expansion, planned to use his noggin to get rich and laid at the same time.

Perhaps because he had dabbled unsuccessfully in a number of careers from acting to land speculating, he found it to his advantage to court her as an adventurer with a mysterious past. He went so far as to claim inside information pertaining to the mysterious suicide of the famous explorer Meriwether Lewis, but would not reveal it. He was dashing in a blunt sort of way that Pippa found amusing. He recounted gruesome events, in such exotic locales as Key West and Kentucky, in such an understated manner that she felt brave just listening to him.

In his dealings with Backhouse Fish Lippencot, Slant hinted at pirate treasure and claimed that common sense, not education, had gotten him where he was today. College, he said to Backhouse's great disdain, was nothing more than a hideout for the indecisive and he was happy to have had none of it. All of which was showboat on his part as records show that Slant was the third son of an elegant Virginia tobacco buyer and extremely well schooled for his time.

The courtship came to a head, so to speak, at a picnic on the beach at Rockaway. After chivalrously not crowding Pippa under the shade of her parasol, Slant feigned a sun-induced headache and got her to rub his brow. Being a curious woman, her slender fingers were soon embarked on phrenological explorations above his hairline. Science is so interesting. Almost immediately she discovered that he had the lumps of a genius.

18/For the Baby's Sake

Round and round in that old gravitation of love and money went Pippa and Slant, while New York society fluttered with catty speculation as to his motives and her sanity. Old Backhouse paid little attention until he was informed that both Thomas Jefferson and John Adams had died on the same day, July 4, 1826, which just happened to be the same day that his only offspring had married. And looking back over that week he recalled fizzling fireworks on the nation's rainy birthday and thought dark hopeless thoughts about middle-age marriages. They were better than no marriages to be sure, but they were about as American as being broke.

Anticipating the worst, he nonetheless gave his daughter and her husband a red brick house, with stables, just off the Washington Military Parade Ground, and hoped for the best. The best being a grandson.

No problem if you know how to go about it, and the newlyweds seemed to. Not that she had the sweet flesh of cherries under her tongue, but Pippa was sweet enough and Slant got right to it. They drank a lot of sherry and screwed in the afternoons. Evenings they went on the town in rounds of boisterous dinner bouts with whoever could keep up. Pippa had the money and Slant definitely had the time.

They would return home after such evenings and take brandy to bed, where Pippa would insist that they make love in French. Slant would go along on the condition that in the morning, when he inevitably woke up hung over and horny, they make love like animals. Lions one morning, whales the next, and so on. Pippa preferred unicorns.

Then it happened, as it often does between men and women who think of their life together as theatre: she became pregnant and everything changed, soured. She quit drinking and he took up the slack.

What's the deal? Slant wanted to know.

Our life is no life for a child, she said. Your life is no life for a father. Don't spill on the carpet, I'm tired of things spilling on carpets. My carpets.

Slant whipped out his thing and pissed his initials on the carpet.

Let me tell you about a dream I had, Pippa said. There was this graveyard on what looked like a beach and there were many new graves and they were all unmarked except one. Yours.

What's that supposed to mean?

Needless to say, they began arguing like gypsies. Make that existential gypsies. Worse, she began prefacing everything she said to him with *for the baby's sake,* and was quite blunt with her opinion that it was no big deal to father a son (she had a feeling about that). The true test of manhood was making something of yourself that a son (that feeling again) could look up to.

For the baby's sake, at least get a job.

He'd show her. He took a position as social columnist with the New York *Sun* and was soon thrashing friends of the family in print. The *ooh la la* and animal noises disappeared forever from their bed and Slant began frequenting a neighborhood cathouse kept at demanding standards by one Madame Josie Spoon. There, surrounded by feathers, music, coquettish conversation, and good champagne, he found love. Not good, sticky, carnal love, although he did do his duty, as Josie called it, with all of her jaunty girls at least once. Slurping and sliding had nothing to do with it, this new love of Slant's. It grew, rather, from imagination—his and Josie's. And it began as a parlor game they invented together the first time he walked in.

What can I do for you?

How about a miracle, Slant said, disgusted with women in general.

Of the flesh or spirit?

Whichever is the more difficult for you to manage, he told her.

How would you like to meet an earth angel, she

winked, one with the bloom of Eden and the grace of a swan on a silver lake?

Interesting, Slant admitted, warming to the challenge. But what about the fluid moves of a racehorse and the radiance of midnight orchids.

Of course, she replied. And don't forget the elegance of a diamond needle and the purity of an albino's tear.

What fun it was: they leapfrogged in the above manner late into the night, and then nightly well into the months of Pippa's pregnancy. Without a thought to the expectant mother, these two verbal libertines constructed new declensions of hyperbole in the name of an ideal that went far beyond breasts like twin roes hanging out on Mount Gilead. What to name their evolving perfection was a problem until Slant came across an obscure sixteenth-century tract about a western island in the zone of terrestrial paradise that the author, a visionary named Ordonez de Montalvo, had peopled with a race of Amazons ruled by a queen he called Calafia. The queen's name was as tacky as Athena, but one of her huntresses, a canny woman-child who ran with the griffins, had a name that struck Slant's fancy. As you can probably guess, the name was Taya.

What could Pippa do? Her fool of a husband was out till all hours, returning, it seemed, only to moan for someone named Taya in his stupefied sleep. She had no choice but to employ a private agent to follow her husband, and ultimately pay off Josie Spoon to permanently eighty-six him. Josie was happy enough to oblige in this regard, saying that things were getting a bit kinky anyway. From that point until he left New York for keeps, Slant spent most of his time drinking alone on his roof, staring west, toward Newark and beyond.

I must soon quit this scene, he told himself upon seeing his son T. D. Jr. born ugly and screaming like a troll.

I am considering an affair, Pippa confided to the little Frenchman who owned the haberdashery where she bought white knit suits for the baby.

It was just a matter of time.

19/For the Baby's Sake II

The wealth of furs that had changed hands at the Great Salt Lake had by this time reached the eastern markets, and numerous expeditions were being organized to cash in on the newly opened territory. To the courageously greedy and the morose, a trek west made infinitely more sense than waiting around to be hit by a pack of escapees from the Fifth Avenue Home for the Reformation of Juvenile Delinquency or taking the train out to Hoboken to watch a shaggy old sack of bones get croaked in one of the lately popular buffalo hunts that drew thousands of New Yorkers. At least that's how Slant saw things.

Thus, he angled an opportunity to join up with a company of uncertain sponsorship led by Benjamin Louis Bonneville. Slant would serve as historian and record keeper with the rank of lieutenant. The hardest part, he sarcastically informed his colleagues at the paper, would be deciding what to wear.

When he informed his wife that he would be stepping out for a couple of years *for the baby's sake,* she replied caustically that if he had to run away to act like a man he might as well not come back. They never saw each other again.

His departure on a muggy August morning, on the first of what turned out to be a number of expeditions, left her in a rather comfortable balance. She had T. D. Sr. to hate and she had T. D. Jr. to love.

Although little is known about her romantic life after her husband ran off, it is probably safe to assume that she screwed around. There was a great deal of gossip about her, and she started drinking sherry again in the afternoon.

20/T. D. Jr.

The privilege and protection afforded T. D. Slant Jr. as a child did not stop him from tumbling out of his adolescence with a certain, well, hunger. He entered Harvard College at seventeen and threw himself into a full flowering of collegiate decadence. He hung around with a club of rich southern boys and distinguished himself as a foul-mouthed rascal on club outings through Boston's waterfront brothels and dives. In his sophomore year he smoked opium on a bet.

Pippa Lippencot Slant naturally did all she could for her son, and old Backhouse in turn promised wondrous rewards if the lad would just settle down and study. But it was no use. T. D. Jr. found class-work the equal of floggings, and the suffocating or-thodoxies of scholarly Cambridge, he claimed, made him at times want to puke his guts out.

He had the temperament of an artist, Pippa de-cided. She encouraged him to study art, and as it turned out he was not without talent. He could sketch easily and well, often capturing the complex-ities of landscape with an economy of strokes. He dropped out of Harvard but remained in Boston, tak-ing a large empty warehouse near the docks as a studio. His paintings were considered stark.

He was disgusted with the romanticism of con-temporary painting, all those rainbows and lapdogs with pink bows around their necks, the dripping sentiment and cute symbolism and sloppy drafts-manship. He rebelled. He became obsessed with re-alism. He tried to paint scenes exactly as he saw them but his talent failed him. He simply could not catch life in a mirror.

But all was not lost. He had been following the development of daguerreotype and now began to see it as reality's main chance. The process was clumsy, requiring a bulky camera box, long exposures during which there could be no movement, and the compli-cated and precise juggling of silver, sunlight, and various chemical vapors at specific temperatures; but the results were splendid. There were portrait stu-dios employing the process, turning out likenesses so accurate that you could count a man's whiskers.

T. D. Jr. soon mastered the technique, but not to make portraits. He was determined to bring its realism to landscapes, to turn the lens on the world and show what it looked like, what it really looked like with no pussyfooting around. He was interested in perspective and the scale of things, images too grand for the normal eye to register without help, pictures so real yet of such sweeping scope that they became abstract, like the horizon or the future. He wanted to put man in his place.

Massachusetts, indeed all of the East, let T. D. Jr. down. Nowhere could he find views of sufficient depth to test his principles.

He was cursing the tininess of it all in a saloon near his studio on the occasion of his twenty-first birthday, when he met Richard Henry Dana. Dana, the eccentric and bumbling attorney who, as a Harvard undergraduate, had shipped before the mast to California and written a best seller about it. Poor Dana, now so pitifully under the thumb of a pious Calvinist wife that he was forced to cloak his visits to the joints on the waterfront in the guise of missionary work. T. D. Jr. had read the book and saw him coming.

Young man, Dana demanded in a stern and fatherly voice, what business have you in this dive and what is that evil you are drinking?

He snatched up T. D. Jr.'s drink and put it away in one neat swallow. T. D. Jr. ordered another drink for Dana to sample and, remembering that the best humor is based on cruelty, decided to have a little fun.

So . . . it's come to this, T. D. Jr. goaded.

What's come to what?

Old men in dry months waiting for pain.

What?

Like you, T. D. Jr. said, waiting for pain. You know, out of it. Why don't you quit playing the fool?

Dana was incredulous. Veins bulged in his forehead. His eyes narrowed. He stared at his hands now gone parchment grey after years of association with little other then ledgers and holy scriptures. Then, slowly squeezing them into soft fists, he looked up at T. D. Jr. and blurted out what would catch on a century later as a truly all-American response: I could have had it all.

Sure, T. D. Jr. said, rolling his eyes. But he did sense a certain change fibrillating in Dana. A temporary change to be sure, but at least notable in that Dana started buying his own drinks. And as he drank on, Dana's imagination took giant steps backward, which in turn hoisted his dignity like a flag, until he was swaggering at the bar like a buccaneer. Gesturing wildly with his walking stick, he raved about his adventures as a young man, depicting heroic scenes of himself in California, a land of such enormous presence as to dwarf God's own soul . . . but not his.

Not knowing any better, T. D. Jr. was intrigued, and they drank together through the night, an old man telling a young man about fortune and mistakes, lying.

At dawn the sun popped up out of the Atlantic, splattering them straight in the face with what Dana translated to T. D. Jr. as the moral of what they had been talking about. With tears in his eyes, Dana said that a man's only business was to make his life as exciting and interesting as possible.

Go to California, he said, and don't come back.

Why not, T. D. Jr. figured, maybe the place had scale.

21/The Artist's Progress

T. D. Jr. returned to New York and told his mother that he was going west to make his life more interesting. He felt his boots quite solid on the marble floor of his mother's library.

California, he said.

Pippa looked at her son standing there in his bottle-green cutaway and thought the scariest thought a mother can think: I have birthed a fool.

Naturally she was bitter, figuring that her son's plans had something to do with the rumor she had heard about her estranged husband having settled in California. But this was not the case; it had nothing to do with his father although, now that she mentioned it, looking old T. D. up once he got there sounded like a reasonable thing for T. D. Jr. to do.

Dinner that evening with Backhouse Fish Lippencot went badly. Pippa soon exhausted reasonable argument and grew snide and bitchy. T. D. Jr. stared at the cherubs and stags molded into the ceiling, and nervously drummed his butter knife on the stemware. Old Backhouse looked alternately at his daughter and grandson and thought it was all too predictable for words. It figures, is all he would say.

Finally, in desperation, Pippa gave T. D. Jr. a copy of his father's book so that he could read for himself of the scoundrels Dad had taken up with. T. D. Jr. said he'd read it on the way, and after spending the money his grandfather had slipped him on the best daguerreotype equipment and chemicals available, he traveled west by rail and stage to St. Louis. There he boarded a paddle-wheel gambling boat and enjoyed the cruise down the Mississippi immensely, winning close to $1,000 at roulette with what the croupier, one Pierre Wallingsford, described as blind luck.

Disembarking in New Orleans, however, he was approached by Wallingsford, who explained that he had ensured the young traveler's luck by clever manipulation of a hidden foot pedal. Wallingsford claimed to have been fired as a result and now expected his share of the winnings. T. D. Jr. questioned Wallingsford's honesty and in the ensuing argument the latter challenged the former to a duel. They were to meet in a meadow curtained with weeping willows and Spanish moss at dawn the following day, but T. D. Jr. made other arrangements.

He cleared the harbor shortly after midnight aboard a dark-sailed bark of dubious reputation bound for Panama, leaving Wallingsford's underhanded deal with the dueling referees to cause more trouble and embarrassment for the former croupier.

T. D. Jr. was disgusted to find that his ship, the *Rainbow*, was a former outlaw vessel only recently gone straight as a slaver. When a storm splintered her mizzenmast eleven days out of New Orleans, forcing her into Vera Cruz for repairs, he sought other transportation as a protest against human bondage. The captain called him a naive lickspittle and refused to refund any portion of his fare. Undaunted, T. D. Jr. decided upon a land crossing of Mexico and reached Mazatlan two months later with a respectable command of Spanish, a bleached mustache, and a deep tan.

Leaving Mazatlan he sailed for Monterey via the Sandwich Islands, a roundabout route only to those who don't understand the ass-busting monotony of a long tack up the coast. During the layover in Honolulu he made several daguerreotypes of spectacular volcanic mountains and a portrait of one Samuel Brannan, the leader of a party of quarrelsome Mormons, also en route to California. Apparently something about Brannan fascinated him.

Under sail again on the last leg of his journey, young T. D. watched dolphins racing the bow of the schooner *Eagle* and counted the days like a spoiled child waiting for his birthday.

FIVE

22/Joaquin Peach

Sexual currents and horses, fandangos in the plaza, and sweet kisses on the beach; but not for Taya.

The *Eagle* was in from the Sandwich Islands and Taya watched naked Worm Eaters pile hides on the embarcadero. The *Eagle* was rumored to have two violins in its hold along with its stocks of coffee, chocolate, and gun powder, and there was much excitement. Any excuse for a *baile*. Taya had dressed carefully in her best deerskin boots, embroidered chemise, and full, gathered muslin skirt secured about her waist with a scarlet silk sash. Dressing up improved her mood but she had no plan for dancing. No, she had come to watch the way things happen to people.

Two greaser dons in from San Juan Bautista for some shopping strutted toward her. They wore their britches part way open to show off full underdrawers of white linen. Separating in front of her like a river current sliding around a snag, they passed close on either side making obscene high-pitched sucking sounds. As they melded side-by-side again behind her, she turned to spit, but it was no use. They were laughing. She bit her lip and walked back across the plaza toward the custom house.

Everywhere there was preparation for the baile, and everywhere also there was talk of revolution against Mexico and speculation about take-over by the gringos. Gringos, of course, were known as good dancers but Taya didn't think about them that way anymore. She had been having her own revolution. She had begun to think of herself as a country, her own country, a free country, the United States of Herself. And such sovereignty not only saved her spirit; it was perfect for California back then. Indeed, the land was peppered with assorted free-state personas looking to increase their treasuries.

Near the customhouse she was confronted by just such a person, one Joaquin Peach, formerly of Valpariso. He wore the billowy white pants of his native Chile and carried himself with the confidence of a conquistadore. He had come to California to soldier for Mexico but, seeing the possibilities, quickly struck out on his own with a number of other *rotos*. The rotos, of course, were a class apart, men with much tradition. Originally the lowborn gangsters who had driven Spain out of Chile, new generations of rotos had gone on to fight for various ambitious politicians in revolution after revolution throughout South America. Now they were showing up in California, gay and belligerent, starting knife fights and stealing chickens.

Well, here comes the sunshine, Joaquin Peach announced loudly as Taya approached.

I hate you all, Taya thought, and kept walking.

Wait, Peach said, I saw you with those greaser dons. How about a present?

As she passed, Peach smiled and reached out for her arm. Taya slapped his hand away. He smiled again. She went and leaned against a barrel in the shade of a fat oak on the edge of the plaza. Peach followed her.

Please wait, he said. And watch. Fun for you, and a present too. Maybe.

A quick bow and he was off, swaggering through the scattered crowd toward the two greaser dons who were now celebrating their purchase of twin tortoise-shell combs from the schooner's mate. They were taking turns gulping from a bottle of brandy and flashing the combs at passing Californianas, with lecherous suggestions as to how the combs might be had. Obnoxious but altogether common behavior for gentlemen of their class.

Taya watched Joaquin Peach step between them and in one quick flurry snatch the bottle and rap them both on the forehead. They went down like puppets with their strings cut and Peach picked up the combs. Speed and surprise were of the essence here, but Peach did not rush off. Instead, he stood proudly exhibiting the combs. A crowd gathered. The greaser dons worked at blinking their way out of the shock that always follows a sucker punch. It took them about a minute to focus on Peach; and it was at this point that Peach told them they had the manners of goats and turned on his heel in the direction of his horse. The chase was on.

Chase, however, is the wrong word. Follow-the-leader would be more like it. Around the plaza went Peach, picking up more mounted pursuers with each pass. And soon he was doing tricks, gallop bounces and saddle reverses, which all in his dust, including the greaser dons, found impossible to resist mimicking. Or improving on.

This showboating merry-go-round went on for a good ten minutes, until Peach dropped the tortoise-shell combs in front of Taya, and hit the road north at a high lope with the greaser dons et al in whooping pursuit.

How dashing.

But so what. Taya picked up the combs and tossed them into a small huddle of Worm Eaters. She'd take a ride herself.

Trotting south down the beach toward the point, she hardly noticed a young man with a pale mustache messing around with strange devices and holding forth at the *Eagle*'s captain about the significance of what he had just seen. Something about a tool for dealing with things everybody knows about but isn't attending to, and something more about his work catching things you don't usually see.

No, Taya hardly noticed.

23/Family Portrait

T. D. Jr. had a picture of his father, a daguerreotype actually, that he had made from a family portrait he found in the attic of his mother's townhouse. He had studied it until he was convinced that he could recognize his father anywhere, but standing at the patio gate that evening in California he was not so sure.

Excuse me.

The old man was obviously drunk. He located the sound easily enough but seemed to have difficulty shifting his eyes to fix the young intruder in his liquid vision.

I am looking for Mr. T. D. Slant.

What's it to you?

T. D. Jr. tried to measure the deterioration of the old man. He moved closer in the twilight, close enough to catch a whiff of whisky breath vaporizing with the essence of rose water and the smell of beard wax and damp tobacco. And something else. The scent of bile, perhaps, sweating through the old man's pores. It was vaguely familiar. He had sniffed it as an infant in a white knit suit crawling through dirty laundry. Suddenly he was sure.

Father!

The old man's eyes twitched frantically, out of control, flooding. Could this really be his son, the son he had walked away from like a bad debt? No. More likely just another rude joke meant to humiliate him further. And yet, if it were true, if the young man standing before him truly was his son, what better time for him to arrive? A son in need is a son indeed, he reasoned. Still, he'd be damned if he'd let this kid, son or not, make a fool of him.

Prove it!

T. D. Jr. pulled the daguerreotype from his coat pocket and handed it to the old man. Sure enough. Captured in the silver emulsion, a woman sat with a slight curl to her mouth. An infant in a knit suit of obvious French styling balanced on her lap. Standing behind them was a man in a beaver hat. Old T. D. Slant squinted and found himself locking eyes with one of the men he used to be.

A moment later, he passed out.

24/Taya

Taya rode the beach late into the night, watching the tide pull the sand clean then wash back and mess it up again. It occurred to her that she was no longer living her life. That it was the other way around. That her life was living her.

25/Youth Wants to Know

When Taya found father and son together on the patio in the morning, much explaining was in order all the way around. T. D. Jr. agreed. He had liked her right off, when he had seen her in the plaza. And he liked her more now. Taya made breakfast and then sat next to T. D. Jr. across from the old man. Together they waited.

You know how it is when someone doesn't want to tell quite the whole truth? Well, that was old T. D., his mind strobing back over the years, looking for easy answers. He felt a babbling fit coming on, and there was no dignity in that. Taya kept staring at him as if he were someone else, and his son, he noticed, wasn't blinking much either. He lost his wits totally for a long silent moment and when they returned he was desperate.

What do you want from me?

T. D. Jr. was a bit unnerved by the outcry but Taya wasn't even startled. Her words came out flat and sharp.

Who is he?

Who?

My father.

It was not as if she were deliberately hardening on old T. D. Or was she? He had expected her to ask, eventually, when they were both recovered, but not now. When he saw something very sharp crystallizing in her eyes he went to pieces and told her everything he knew. Almost.

And strange, very strange was the following week. Almost no conversation among the three of them, but they were very polite to each other, like new in-laws. Finally, off they went, leaving Monterey in a wet predawn fog. First Taya and T. D. Jr. riding out front on horseback. Then came old Slant, creaking along in a small cart loaded with the books he was

saving for his old friend Vallejo, a few personal ef-
fects, and his son's daguerreotype paraphernalia.

Over the years, old T. D. had developed a theory
about the four points of the compass. You go west
for adventure, east for civilization, south for hospi-
tality, and north for obscurity. He sucked in the
damp air and exhaled a low gushing whistle. Whew,
he was traveling north. What he saw as the new
inevitabilities of his life eased through his mind, and
he relaxed at the prospect of fading quietly into in-
significance. He was kidding himself.

And he was still at it when they reached the scattered fruit orchards of the Santa Clara Valley. They
stopped beside a shiny little creek and he suggested
they rest for an hour or so, take a little nap. Without
waiting for an answer, he arranged himself in the
warm grass and stared up at a blank, indifferent sky.
But before he could close his eyes, Taya sent the twin
horses of guilt and anxiety racing through his mind
once again by announcing that she was not going on
to Yerba Buena.

She said she was going to find her father and then
take care of Sewey and the Burgetts. She had decided, and that was that. He and T. D. Jr. here could
do as they pleased. She had crows to pluck.

Old T. D. rattled to his feet, arguing like an auc-
tioneer, spitting a combination of perils and insecur-
ities at her like darts. He called her an hysterical
adolescent. He spit in the creek for emphasis. It was
the worst of times and dangerous folly to go traipsing
around in this obviously darkening climate looking
for a father who was, likely as not, dead anyway.

When he ran out of argument he threatened her with force. Goddamnit, he'd make her stay with him, for her own good. But when she calmly shook her head, he found himself nodding hopelessly in uneasy agreement.

T. D. Jr., who had remained silent through his father's harangue, was now about to offer up similar advice when she turned to him, a cautious smile unfolding on her face like a challenge, and he could not stop himself from returning it. After all, it was a man's business to make her life as exciting and interesting . . . etc. He liked her better than his father anyway: youth against age, and all that. Maybe even a bit more.

That evening in San Jose, old T. D. told Taya about Counsel, the only man he thought might know what had passed over the last fifteen years with Buckdown. And later that night he took his son aside. They walked out into the warm darkness of the town's deserted square, mind to mind, father and son perhaps for the first time. Perhaps for the only time. They kept their voices low, specific, and sentimental.

The next morning old T. D. Slant climbed into his cart and headed for Yerba Buena alone, wondering if Buckdown was alive and asking himself if courage had to hang between a man's legs.

SIX

26/Buckdown

Buckdown had cut the moorings of his life as simply as he cut loose the martin and beaver he found still alive in his traps. He put none out of misery, even as he found them gnawing through their own shanks toward freedom. He simply set them free and watched numbly as they limped away, dragging maimed paws and forelegs in shock. He ate the dead ones out of habit but left their pelts where they fell like so many bloody rags to stiffen in the weather.

When he wanted to talk he would go find Counsel's place, wherever it happened to be at the time, on the Great Salt Lake one year, back up on the Yellowstone the next. He would take months searching it out, wanting to talk out the string of his pathetic life. But then he would get there and have nothing to say. Counsel had a Shoshone wife. That was part of it. And Counsel guarded her jealously.

The last time Buckdown visited Counsel it was winter, snowing at Counsel's new place on the Snake. He found the trader deep in conversation with Hippolyte Weed. They were talking about California, where Weed was heading.

Milk and honey and furs and fun,
California, here I come.

Weed kept repeating his rhyme, while Counsel insisted that he couldn't care less.

Once again Buckdown could find nothing to say and left at once without even a peek at Counsel's wife. Tears froze on his cheeks and he was glad the falling snow was covering his tracks. He would be gone from the world of men. Yes. And women?

His wife was past him, he knew that, but her death pulled at him with each dropping moon. He couldn't think. He made up simple equations in his mind, but none of them balanced. He loved her, still loved her, and that was the terrible weight of his unbalanced reckoning. He had led her and that bastard Slant on an expedition that scouted too deep into the wilds of happiness. It was all his fault. He hated himself. The seasons rolled by around him. He lost years.

27/His Own Ghost

Buckdown became a wandering recluse, traveling aimlessly, talking only to animals. He was a strange

man and strange things happened. One day, staring
over some nameless cliff. . . .

Brother!

Buckdown jerked around to face a grinning collage
of bones, feathers, and vegetation. It was His Own
Ghost, the albino son of a minor subchief of the
tricky Western Utes. As a child his unique opaque-
ness had marked him for a life of spiritual pursuits
with no questions asked. He was considered gifted,
a prodigy. At twelve he was recognized as a full-rank
shaman, by fourteen he was experimenting with medicinal plants, and at fifteen he had hit the trail less
traveled by. Now in his fortieth spring, as he put it,
he was widely known as a keeper of the spiritual
buckskins. He traveled from tribe to tribe, from the
Colorado to the Klamath, spreading visionary in-
sights and potent little peyote buttons that he gathered and processed in his own secret desert near
Agua de Las Vegas.

In Buckdown he recognized a man obviously ajar
with himself, but a man with a certain potential for
mythic content just the same. He had been following
the mountainman for several weeks, noting his peculiar behavior and intense sorrow.

I am His Own Ghost and I was born magic, he told
Buckdown. Sit down and relax. I will put you
straight.

Buckdown blinked. There he was, eye to eye with
a pink-eyed Indian, being offered salvation as if it
were a piece of dog meat. His jaw dropped and His
Own Ghost thrust a carved bone pipe into the gaping
mouth. Why not? Buckdown figured, and puffed.
His Own Ghost smiled and fired up a pipe for him-

self. The wind rose. They sat down smoking, studying each other.

Buckdown wondered about His Own Ghost's outfit. His footwear had been fashioned from two large desert reptiles, lizards slit down the back and hollowed out to accommodate feet. The dragonlike heads and heavily scaled tails had been left intact. They wiggled at heel and toe of the shaman's feet as if about to take off in directions of their own choice. His loins were packed with some kind of elemental muck, wet and pliable, yet concrete enough to support an assortment of flowering twigs and branches that had been poked, or perhaps planted, into it. Over his shoulders he wore a cape of white feathers, ribbed with the delicate skeletons of tiny rodents and snakes. It gave off a hollow tinkling sound whenever His Own Ghost moved his arms. Hanging from his neck were a number of brightly colored pouches.

Good smoke, Buckdown said.

Tolache, His Own Ghost corrected. Some people call it jimsonweed and ignore the white flowers that blow everywhere. Stupid and sad people, the Great Emptiness for them.

Buckdown didn't know what to think. He himself felt stupid and sad. Then he began to feel little feathers growing out of his head and he wanted to fly with the birds. His Own Ghost kept him on the ground.

I have seen you be kind to the animals, the shaman said, and that is okay as far as it goes. But you are not one of the Animal People so don't kid yourself. Live like a man. Have some fun. Otherwise your path will sneak up on you from behind.

Buckdown wasn't sure. He wanted to tell His Own Ghost a tall and outrageous lie. Say what a big shot he could be if he felt like it. Instead he held out the pipe for more tolache.

You feel like lying, His Own Ghost said, refilling both pipes. That's a sign. Tolache is clever. She will cure you for a while, but she can kill you just as easy, so this is all you get.

When his second pipe was finished Buckdown was nervous and sad. And mad. His Own Ghost grinned at him.

Now you're getting it. Men should be mad not sorry. Now go live with your own kind someplace and pay attention. Look for a sign. If you get shaky take one of these.

His Own Ghost removed one of the pouches from his neck and tossed it down to Buckdown.

What's this? Buckdown fumbled it open and squinted inside at a dozen hard little orbs.

Each one has a spirit. If the spirit likes you she will help you. Otherwise, watch out. Good luck, and look me up if you run out.

With that His Own Ghost took off, the lizards bobbing with his hurried steps, tiny vertebrae rattling in his cape.

Buckdown sank into a clear sleep, wondering why the afternoon sun was taking on a blue haze and what had happened to his feathers. Everything else seemed obvious. How long he slept remains a mystery.

When he woke he felt like someone had left his bones out in the rain. His joints ached. His muscles felt like saturated sponges. And there was something else, a tingle, a not unpleasant shiver in his tired old body. He stretched and decided to head west, as far west as he could go.

California, here he comes. . . .

28/Fort Ross

It was 1835. Buckdown came careening into what he thought was Monterey. Wrong. Instead of gentle padres and coy señoritas he found a handful of foul-breathed Russians lording over perhaps a hundred wild Aleutians and a pack of expert pelt hunters from Kodiak Island. The czar had dispatched them to California to raise crops for his starving colony in Sitka and to satiate, if they could, the boundless hunger for soft otter fur that was gnawing at his economy from St. Petersburg to the Ukraine. They were also supposed to keep an eye on the Spanish, the French, the British, the Americans, and anybody else found pirating around on his Pacific Rim.

Before Buckdown realized his mistake, he found himself surrounded. The Russians put him through a round of suspicious pleasantries and insisted that he stay for a while.

Followed closely by several pellet-eyed Aleutians who grinned at him with wooden teeth whenever he turned around, Buckdown spent the afternoon sniffing in the fishy wind, checking things out. Bales of otter pelts were stacked about in great quantity as they overflowed from a rough log tannery, but the crops on the small cleared plain behind the fort were withered and failing.

Buckdown walked north along the cliff. Kayaks needled in and out of the surf on the beach below, dropping off furry, wet bundles of dead weight. The tide churned like a reaper, sucking delicate and disturbingly childlike carcasses off what Buckdown figured to be the skinning beach. The next thing he knew it was dinner time. Somewhere someone was ringing a bell.

The Aleutians hustled Buckdown into a stuffy room, steeped with the smell of fish oil. He was eyeing the first course, salmon eggs and acorns, when one of the Russians mumbled something to the Aleutian at the door and another guest was led into the dining room. Buckdown had never seen anyone like him. The man's face was as flat as the moon, with razor slits for eyes, and no whiskers. His body seemed to have been somehow compacted, foreshortened from the top down by enormous pressure. Yet there was something almost elegant about him, and a jumping intelligence in his pie face.

And he was clean, exotically clean and turned out in such neatness as to appear to have no business whatsoever among his reechy dinner companions. While they were draped in ill-fitting skins and coarse wool, he wore silk. Heavy and somewhat faded silk, but silk nonetheless. Buckdown was so unfamiliar with such finery that he failed to realize that the man was, in fact, wearing a uniform.

To Buckdown's surprise the Russians seemed far more interested in himself than in their other guest.

They asked question after question, ignoring the strange little man except to grunt at him from time to time. He sat silently working his way through the food with an economy of movement and a total absence of emotion while Buckdown answered questions.

After dinner, the Russians drank themselves pragmatically toward stupefication. Buckdown excused himself and walked down to the beach. He watched the tide go out. Moonbeams glanced metallically off slick pink otter flesh tumbling skinless in the whitewater. Time passed. He might have drifted into a daze. The next thing he knew, the Russians' other guest was standing next to him on the sand.

Help me escape from all this, said the strange little man.

Help me, Buckdown said, without turning.

29/Dead Animals

Buckdown cleared the fort just before dawn. He rode north, through groves of redwood throwing century-length shadows toward the dunes. He did not stop until it was time to stare west, into the fifteen hundred and first sunset since his wife died.

Curious, no wind on the cliff. Just the forest ticking behind him as he watched the sun fall behind the ocean's flat horizon. The spookiness of the trees came over him with a scent of wet bark and a flash of vertigo that sat him down abruptly on the ground.

He pulled the small pouch from around his neck

and emptied it. The small grey buds spilled out. They reminded him of teeth. He ate one: bitter, but a trace of menthol, like a green pinecone. He ate another and mounted up. Hi-Ho Buckdown, riding a delicate passage north along the darkening coast.

At night, the eyes of furry little animals, now dead, are the blackest holes in the universe; but then what is the difference between Buckdown and the stars? This is what Buckdown wonders. And do the stars talk to each other? Only when he is not listening. Then what do the trees eat? The secrets the stars drop. Are the secrets pretty? Some look like rain. How does Buckdown know all this? He drinks some of the secrets when the stars aren't looking.

The balance of his mind is disturbed. Suddenly he wants to piss in the ocean. He has a definite need. It is very important to the stars.

He jumps to the ground and runs off over the dunes. The moon moves behind a cloud. Buckdown stumbles. Now he crawls, wiggling sinewy legs from his musky leggings. Up again, naked now to the waist, he prances into the surf. Foam swirls around his hips. The surge washes his stomach. He squirts his yellow stream beneath the surface. Invigorating. He throws his face toward the sky and whoops, but he might be sorry. Something tells him he is not alone. Dropping low in the dark salty water, Buckdown scans the surf.

The moon slides out again, like a beacon, and he sees some kind of beast, awash to the withers, ambling toward him out of the sea. Buckdown blows a long anxious breath from his lungs and sniffs back the onshore wind. He smells it, that sweet mush of chlorophyll crystallizing to tartar on grazing molars, and green grasses rotting in a fat cud. Buffalo!

Buffalo swimming? Son-of-a-buck!

Buckdown bolts from the tide and sprints back to his pony. His trusted old Hawken rifle, unused for years, waits in its scabbard. He yanks it free and turns back toward the beach. Witness the hunter! Squinting down the cold barrel, he stalks straight away for the ton and a half of muscle and wet shag lowing ashore in the moonlight.

A peculiar game of chicken ensues. Step by step they come together on the sand. And when man and beast were almost close enough to count each other's parasites, something very, well, something very *odd* happened.

30/Buffalo Level

Don't shoot, said the buffalo.

Now there have always been those unable to believe any but the most documented of incidents, and in this case they may have a point. There were no witnesses. Who can truly know if the buffalo was who he said he was or, for that matter, if he spoke at all? Buckdown may have hallucinated the whole thing the same way a self-doubter might construct an elaborate future for himself once he tastes the sauce of official approval. But you never know. Maybe Buckdown tasted something that came from the belly of the land itself.

Anyway.

Anyway, what a brutal and woeful saga the beast unfolded. Classic tragedy, it stretched like a panorama of nobility undone by its own handsome strength. Buckdown listened, rocking in his own body like an infant in a mother's arms. It broke his heart, and the next morning Buckdown followed the buffalo on foot, swallowing gobs of guilt, hump filet memories from the great plains. Once he and Counsel had run maybe a thousand head off a gorge. When it was over they stood silently on the edge, looking down on a pyramid of braying, broken-backed, disjointed agony.

In two days the pyramid had turned into a swarming hill of maggots. The stench lasted for weeks, stretching fifteen miles down the wind. They never even got to the ones that went over the edge first. And who were those brothers who showed up to help with the skinning?

SEVEN

31/Bear Flaggers

When a gaggle of rowdies calling themselves Bear Flaggers rustled a herd of horses being driven south to Monterey from Vallejo's Petaluma Adobe, the Burgett brothers were right there rustling with the best of them. And when the same gang of freebooters swooped into the town of Sonoma, sending General Vallejo in chains to Sutter's Fort and hoisting a crude flag above the plaza, Galon and Millard distinguished themselves in the looting.

The flag was a soiled and crusted swath of cheap cotton sporting a crudely drawn grizzly bear that most Californios thought resembled a hog. It was meant to give credibility to the formation of a new country and the positions of authority each of the Bear Flaggers announced for themselves in its government.

Galon declared himself Grand Wizard and took to wearing a dress sabre liberated from one of the thirteen Mexican Regulars garrisoned in Sonoma. The sabre was too long for Galon's short legs, and its tip trailed in the dust as he strutted the streets feeling the weight of his new status. As usual, his brother Millard was vacantly confused by events but enthusiastically chose for himself the title of Brother of the Grand Wizard.

Social order broke down throughout the region. The Worm Eaters who had been obediently working the cattle and crops in Sonoma's neighborhing countryside got word that everything had changed and wandered off. And worse, the mission Worm Eaters who had for years seen to the worldly needs of the spiritually inclined, dipping an endless number of strings into vats of bubbling candle tallow and delicately coaxing the mission grapes into decanters of sweet wine, could no longer be motivated.

The old padre in charge was beside himself. He had survived the 1822 revolution and the following period of independence from Mother Spain. While most other missions fell into ruin, he had been able, by cultivating Vallejo, to save a semblance of former affluence in spite of the theoretical freeing of the Worm Eaters and demotion of his mission to the status of parish church. But this new plague of infidels was something else. He perceived it as an assault on all that was holy. He called for the judgment day, and made lists of local heretics for God. When his Worm Eaters started sleeping in, he knew the apocalypse was at hand. His righteousness turned hysterical and he ranted about the plaza, clutching a golden crucifix to his bony breast. The cross flashed in the sun, catching the eye of Galon Burgett, who was lounging near the flagpole.

Hey, preacher! Let's have a look at your necklace.

The old padre whirled in his tracks. He knew that voice, or thought he did.

Methodist Wolf!

The Grand Wizard had no choice in the face of such insolence. Scuffing the padre ahead of him like an empty sack, he rampaged through the chapel. He kicked in the altar and spit on the walls. He sliced the Lord's flickering candles with his sabre and threatened to drown the tempest-tossed old holy man in his own sacrificial wine. It was great fun.

The rest of the Bear Flaggers were naturally delighted and big things were predicted for Galon Burgett, but the incident turned out to be his only official act. On maneuvers in the countryside two days later, the Bear Flaggers ran into a superior force of greasers and, after a brief exchange of gunfire, Galon forfeited his position by deserting.

Galloping off over the sun-drenched hills, he shouted to Millard, riding loyally beside him, that he wasn't feeling well and was tired of public life anyway. When they pulled up in a shaded arroyo to give the horses a blow, Galon said that all he wanted was a long rest for himself. He then emphasized his need for a bit of R and R by puking up some blood. Millard was understandably confused and worried until Galon explained to him that their new country wasn't going to last long anyway.

He was right. When it was only three weeks old

the Bear Flag Republic was conquered by the United States of America.

32/Yerba Buena

It turned into a very American summer in California, especially in Yerba Buena. Captain John Montgomery (U.S.N.) landed a squadron of small boats on the mud flats and trudged to the plaza whistling "The Star-Spangled Banner." Swaggering with the glee of conquest, he raised Old Glory himself and declared that he was taking over for what he called the *U States*. Marines in white gloves kept order without firing a shot. But it was an even bigger deal when a ship of faith carrying more than two hundred Mormons landed several weeks later, thereby almost doubling the population.

The locals gossiped about the excesses of polygamy and it was rumored that thousands of additional Mormons were on the way.

Old T. D. Slant considered all this from points of churlish vantage. Deballed at sixty-five, he found himself reduced to the pursuit of the simplest and most insipid of vices. He became a voyeur, a peeping poltergeist of the most lecherous ilk, and although he was very pleased to be in America again, his former interest in current events gave way to earthier preoccupations. He spent time like an old hound, sniffing out the vile indecorums of others, peeking through the cracks and crevices of the new American settlement.

He was especially taken with the notion of cunnilingus, Mormon cunnilingus better yet. He ached to see some gruff old patriarch of the seventh tribe yodeling up vulva canyons, lapping his way around a circle of pious young wives. As it was, only the sad-eyed Worm Eaters were given to such nibblings, and watching them was like watching animals. Mormons would be different, Slant was sure of it.

33/Cargo West

Slant took lodging on Battery Street, a wide dirt promenade that ran along the waterfront. Clearly Yerba Buena's rowdiest strip, it boasted three solid warehouses and one rather attractive structure standing amid a confusion of crumbling mud huts, driftwood sheds, and canvas lean-tos. The handsome building, a two-story wood and adobe arrangement, was known as Cargo West and it was there that Slant felt most at ease.

A combination gentlemen's club, brothel, and hotel, Cargo West was a mecca for buyers and sellers, a place where deals could be made, a place to be. It was never clear who owned controlling interest in the place, although Larkin was sometimes mentioned in this regard. It was, however, very clear that the place was making a lot of money and was frequented by men to be taken seriously.

Evenings, such men would make their way through the riffraff, copulating, drinking, and cheating each other randomly in open shanties, to find civilized fellowship and masculine recreation at Cargo West. Even the most upright, men like Captain John Montgomery (U.S.N.), could be found among the clientele.

Slant took a suite upstairs and for a substantial bribe was permitted by the management to fashion a series of peepholes in his floor. He had one view of the large barroom that occupied a third of the main floor and another of one of the tiny rooms used for more intimate social contact.

Cargo West was run by a low-hipped woman of middle years who was said to have bounced her melon-sized breasts on the shoulders of congressmen as a younger woman in New Jersey. She was a real Wild Emma, in the nomenclature of the period, and was just cocky enough to take up the widespread label for any white woman with a good-time spirit and use it as her own name.

My name is Emma, she would say, greeting newcomers at the door, and I'm the wildest Emma of them all.

Wild Emma was very shrewd, and like all the other women who eventually made fortunes in California, she had no illusions about the men she catered to. Her operation at Cargo West was simple. She employed a sullen Greek with aristocratic manners as head barman and instructed him to make sure that every man taking a drink knew that she, Wild Emma, was indeed the only high-living gringo woman for thousands of miles and that if they expected to be welcome they had best mind their manners.

She filled the tiny rooms off the bar with pretty young Worm Eaters she got from Hippolyte Weed.

They generally lasted anywhere from four to ten months, at which time some were retained as maids. The less fortunate were simply turned out on Battery Street to make do as best they could. Since a tour at Cargo West left almost all of them either hollow-eyed and withdrawn or giddy with dependence on the sweet wine they were encouraged to drink with customers, they usually slid into one of the surrounding three-sided hovels to screw and beg for whatever they could get.

Well, Wild Emma would say if any of her customers turned high-minded about the fate of one or another of the Worm Eaters, you can always marry her. Subject closed.

Wild Emma was suspicious of old T. D. from the beginning. Guests who took upstairs rooms got automatic Worm-Eater privileges along with their board, but all this old fool Slant wanted was to drill holes in the floor. And he walked funny, some kind of Sneaky-Pete for sure.

So Wild Emma was cool toward old T. D. Slant, even when she took his money. Her spinosity, however, did not stop him from enjoying the ambience of Cargo West or taking pleasure at his peepholes. He turned nasty only with the arrival of fresh Worm Eaters. He couldn't resist peeking, of course, and their initiation into brothel life, with Wild Emma giving stern advice, always took something out of him. And the worst part was who some of the Worm Eaters reminded him of.

EIGHT

34/Taya's Map

Time to look at the map. Not the map that T. D. Jr. bought from Larkin when they passed back through Monterey, rather the map that Tanya was charting for herself.

It surveyed no single region, this map, and was useless to look at for truth of area. It was linear, like a map of a road from here to there with no borders except its own width. A map to follow like a tunnel toward a light that, in Taya's case, illuminated Sewey and the Burgetts pleading hopelessly for mercy in the various twisting fates she conjured for them.

Following both maps, they rode south along the coast, day to day from rancho to rancho, through San Simeon and Esteros, over the green hills to San Luis Obispo and on to Santa Inez. Then down into Santa Barbara where the cannon of the old presidio poked seaward over the whitewashed porticos of a small convent.

Taya had seen it all before on trips with old T. D. and was anxious to keep moving, but T. D. Jr. insisted on frequent stops to make daguerreotypes. He had made them all along the coast, pointing his lens off cliffs in all directions, looking for the widest angle, recording landscapes so distant that line and form fell into abstraction, yet catching the tiniest detail on his silver plates. Taya was growing impatient with him and his pumice powder and his mercury vapor and the long waits.

I thought you were going to help me.

He was unloading his camera and coating box from the packhorse on a bluff below the convent. He told her of course he was, but that he also had his work.

Some work.

You don't understand.

You don't.

She threw her face away from him and stared out over the ocean. He shrugged and went about arranging his equipment, engrossed in his work. Several minutes passed before he realized that she was speaking to him again, telling him the story of Concepcion.

35/Dona Concepcion de Arguello

The story of Concepcion was not yet embalmed in legend and Taya had no reverence for it. She simply knew it. As a young girl she had heard it often. She told it to T. D. Jr. like old gossip.

Concepcion was fifteen years old and her father was the commandante then at the presidio near Yerba Buena. They were an important family and many young men liked her and wanted her because she was very beautiful. But she didn't like any of them. Then the count came and she fell in love with him. It was almost fifty years ago.

The count's name was Rezanov and he was a Russian, but he was handsome anyway. He came to trade for food because his people were starving in Sitka. Concepcion's father couldn't trade with him because he didn't think it was right to trade with Russians. Concepcion begged her father to help the count because she was in love with him. When the count found out, he fell in love with her and asked her to marry him. Then there was a lot of trouble because her father was very strict about things and because the count wasn't Catholic.

Concepcion pleaded with her father. She went to her room and would not come out or have anything to eat. The padres came and scolded her but she didn't care. Then the count told her father that he would get permission from the pope and become a Catholic. The padres said that would be fine and her father let them become betrothed and also traded the count what he needed for his people. Then they all had a big fiesta and Concepcion was very happy.

But the count had to go and get permission from the pope like he promised. When he sailed away, Concepcion stood on the beach and blew him kisses. The count promised to write to her from every place he stopped along the way, but no letters came for her. People told her that the count had just loved her so he could trade with her father, but she didn't believe them.

She was very faithful. Fifteen years passed and he didn't come or even send a letter and her father made her become a nun. She cried all the time and was afraid the count was dead, but she was still beautiful. Soon it was too late for everything because her father found out that the count was dead. His horse slipped in a river in Siberia and killed him when he was on his way to see the pope.

When her father came to the convent and told her the count was dead, she didn't believe him. More years passed and she became old and ugly. She still believes the count is coming back to marry her.

The story was over and Taya pointed up the hill toward the convent, it was where Concepcion lived, if she was still alive.

T. D. Jr. didn't know what to say. That's a very sad story, he said.

Concepcion was a fool, Taya told him.

36/Zorro

Out of the night when the full moon was bright there came a horseman known as Zorro.

Taya and T. D. Jr. had been pushing hard to make Agua Caliente before midnight, when the West's first Robin Hood swooped out from behind a big grey rock and got the drop on them with his rapier.

As formidable as he was in his black mask and cape, the gun turned out to be mightier than the sword and Zorro managed to retain the upper hand only until Taya pulled a pistol from her sash.

No fair, Zorro complained, slashing invisible Z's in the air.

The truth of the matter was that Zorro looked like a skinny old bum. This onetime folk hero had fallen upon hard times and had grown senile as the romance of the halcyon days dwindled in what he called the Californias. He had, of course, been hell to pay against the evil Spaniards back when he had lived as the sensitive, mild-mannered Don Diego by day and ridden the wind as Zorro by night. Just ask that fat Sergeant Garcia.

Naturally, T. D. Jr. wanted to make a daguerreotype. He had never made one at night, but the moon was so bright that he figured it was worth a try. The bigger problem would be Zorro, getting him to stand still. It would have to be negotiated. Zorro could obviously use the cash. But before he could broach the subject, who should pop out of the bushes behind them but that flamboyant roto, Joaquin Peach, with the drop on them all.

This is my apprentice, Zorro announced, pointing his rapier at Peach. I'm showing him the ropes.

I thought we'd meet again, Peach said to Taya.

What do you want? she asked.

What do you got? he answered.

Nothing, she said.

Well then, he winked at her, why don't you hang out with me and Zorro for a while?

The Californias are rich, Zorro volunteered. It's

easy to be bad. Bad is good and this is the best island
of all.

We have our own business, said T. D. Jr., trying to
sound tough. He figured he and Peach were about
the same age.

Is that right? Peach asked Taya, ignoring T. D. Jr.

When she said yes, Peach shrugged and explained
the normal procedure. Safe passage over the San Fer-
nando Hills was usually best purchased from him
and Zorro. Otherwise they couldn't be responsible;
and it would be a sad thing if such a fine young
couple fell prey to the hazards of the trail and wound
up completely broke or even dead, like some other
travelers who passed this way just recently.

Ah, come on, Taya said.

Yeah, said T. D. Jr., who do you think you are?
Pizarro or something?

Pizarro, Zorro suddenly shouted. Who's Pizarro?
I'm Zorro.

Yes, we know, Taya told him softly.

There must have been something in the old hero's
desperate outburst or in Taya's response that soft-
ened Peach's attitude. Or maybe he just wanted to
spend a little more time with people his own age. Or
maybe it had all been a big joke anyway. Let's just
talk some more, he said.

And they did: Peach trying to flirt with Taya; Taya
trying to find out if Zorro had ever heard of Buckdown; Zorro trying to explain how things had gone
from bad to worse; and T. D. Jr. trying to explain, as
he set up his equipment, how he would use the
moonlight.

As it turned out, T. D. Jr. did make a daguerreotype, but it was not what he had expected. Zorro had refused to remain in the frame and had instead insisted on watching from a distance of at least ten yards behind T. D. Jr. Completely out of the picture. Yet when the plate was finished, streaks of moonlight angled to form a Z, erasing the features of Taya and Peach, even as their outlines came through clearly.

You'd better watch it, Zorro told T. D. Jr. when all were examining the daguerreotype. Pretty soon everyone will be getting one of these portraits the same way the rich Spaniards used to have themselves painted. And, just like the Spaniards, everyone will look more and more alike.

What he meant was that technology breeds doublecrosses.

Good old Zorro.

37/Pueblo de Los Angeles

Dust, fogged up from hooves of their tired horses, hung above the ground like clouds of brown mist. The faded buildings fronting on the plaza blocked whatever breeze there might have been. It was very hot. The air itself was flat, opaque.

It was almost siesta time and the low-rent Californios lounging here and there in doorways had never heard of Buckdown or Sewey or the Burgetts. When Taya or T. D. Jr. asked about Counsel, the man old T. D. had said would know something, most closed their eyes and would say no more. Finally there was one man, a rather distinguished old Californio in faded blue pants with silver stitching up each leg, who was willing to talk.

Counsel is a mean stupid gringo who can't talk good, he said. We ran him out.

The old Californio was sitting at a table in the shade watching a young Worm Eater coax a small donkey across the otherwise deserted plaza with a stick. The latticework that hung out from the cantina was covered with dry brown vines. It filtered the midday sun and freckled the old man's face with tiny points of shadow. Like most southern Californios, he sensed coercion in any arrangement involving three or more foreigners and enjoyed it very much when they wound up killing each other. He was drinking mescal.

If you want to kill this Counsel, he has a trading store near Tejon on the trail to the San Joaquin, he said. Good luck.

When T. D. Jr. told him that they just wanted to talk to this man Counsel, the old Californio became very agitated. He cursed out at the sun and fumbled in his belt for a pistol which he dropped on the table with a thud. He began talking very fast.

California is almost for dogs, he said, glaring at T. D. Jr. Mexico gives us monte players and cholos. France sends us prostitutes and little bullies. Chile, sneak thieves and rotos. Highway bandits come from Peru and some place called Ireland, probably a prison in England. Italy, pickpockets and bad musicians. Spain's degenerate priests are still here, and you gringos are all politicians and plotters. It is all getting to be the shits.

Taya told the old man that she understood. He paid her back by grabbing at her breasts and moving his hips obscenely below the table. T. D. Jr. snatched up the gun and leveled it at the old Californio's head.

Who do you think you are?

I am the mayor of Pueblo de Los Angeles, the old man shouted. Get out of my town.

38/Peek-a-Boo

Four hundred miles away, Joaquin Peach rode into Yerba Buena looking for bigger things. What kind of backwater trick was this? he wondered. Compared to Valpariso, this Yerba Buena was a dog village. Sweet erb, indeed.

Christ, what a collection of bullshitters all living together in a disgusting summer fog. In Valpariso there was a lighthouse, and white mansions set like pearls among groves of almonds and citrus, and hillside gardens with rows and rows of heliotropes and geraniums. Here he saw only mud flats and weeds. The wind howled over the sharp hills behind him and a shiver chased up his spine like a fine and violent lace.

He had left Zorro in a deserted Worm-Eater camp near the Mission San Antonio de Padua, which was now for sale. The old hero had insisted on keeping track of prospective buyers, hoping no doubt to run into some old ghosts. It was the ghosts that had started to trouble Peach. Zorro was always talking about them; and worse, talking to them. Was that where *duende* led? Duende, that mysterious and ineffable charm of the good outlaw that Zorro more than anyone else had once defined. You sure as hell couldn't spend duende, couldn't even buy an old broken-down mission with it. Poor Zorro, he should have planned ahead. Shit, Peach thought, and here I am in this shit hole. To improve his mood, he went looking to get laid.

Interesting, how all living things seem to suffer postcoital depression, a sadness that sneaks in even after the most brightly colored of screws. Old T. D. Slant made a note of it. He was poised on all fours in his suite at Cargo West, once again squinting through his favorite peephole.

In the room below he could see Joaquin Peach stretched out across the bed like some deposed prince of love. Less than an hour earlier the roto had stomped into Cargo West like a conquistadore just returned from El Dorado with the loot. He had swaggered up to the bar and bellowed intentions to satisfy his various and wide-ranging carnal needs in every imaginable rut. It was then that old T. D. had bought him a drink of encouragement and hurried eagerly to his vantage points on the floor above. What a disappointment.

After less than an hour of undistinguished diddling with a perfectly capable and enterprising young Worm Eater, Joaquin Peach was deep in a funk. He was down, way down, but not because he had performed poorly. For the satisfaction of the

Worm Eater he cared zero. Let her go squat on an anthill. What bothered him was something, shall we say, more universal. He had not been doing well in California so far and this weighed heavily upon him now that his balls were empty. What would Pizarro have done? Joaquin Peach rose from the bed. He dressed slowly, covering his body and, he hoped, his doubts with the care of a matador about to enter the ring. Then he smiled sadly at the Worm Eater and, pants billowing, went back to the bar.

Old T. D. Slant was about to call it a night himself when another man eased into the room. A tall man with a close-clipped beard and nervous hands poking out of stiff-boiled cuffs. Slant recognized him with hand-rubbing relish. It was Brannan.

The Mormon captain examined the sad-eyed little Worm Eater on the bed with clinical thoroughness. He traced and probed his way over her body from top to bottom. He turned her over on her stomach and kneaded her smooth round ass. He turned her over on her back once again and, taking hold of her ankles, spread her legs.

Old T. D. could no longer see Brannan's face. The Mormon had dropped to his knees at the foot of the bed and was groaning between the Worm Eater's thighs. Old T. D. was beside himself with the possibilities. His mind churned in syncopation with Brannan's bobbing head. By chance his eyes wandered up to the Worm Eater's face. It was a mistake. Her eyes grew wider and moved across the ceiling. She locked on Slant's peephole like a timid animal frozen by a torch in the night.

Slant was pinned. He felt tied to all women like the tail of a falling kite.

39/Taya

Dwarf shrubforms clustered here and there in tight packs on the grey underslope of the Tehachapi Mountains. In the moonlight their shadows seemed almost human, apelike, an army of monkeys or midgets standing guard in the night. Taya's mind was a cold garden. She dreamed of growing things, shapes and textures pushing and sliding against each other, trying to break free. And all around her she felt the large movements of men and horses. When they began looking for her she woke up.

She looked across the dying fire at T. D. Jr. He was wide awake, searching among the stars of some inner midnight, waiting for the night to fall away. He looked over at her. They heard a scraping beneath the folded mountains, teeth perhaps, tearing into the earth somewhere under the crust. Without speaking they gathered their gear and saddled the horses. And soon they were climbing again, higher into the mountains, riding out the night together in silence.

NINE

40/Petaluma Adobe

The frontal perspective on Galon Burgett's health was confusing. Sometimes he looked pretty good and sometimes he didn't. His energy seemed to depend on the weather. Heat bothered him and on days like this, with shimmering lines rising from the needle grass and greasewood, he was a ragged quiver of symptoms. He coughed a lot, his eyes turned yellow, and there were irregularities in his stool.

He walked across the courtyard of the huge adobe that had served until recently as the working headquarters for the Rancho Petaluma, with its endless acres and its long-horned cattle by the thousands, its fine horses and its wheat and tallow and wine. It was almost deserted now, most of the Worm Eaters gone back to their scratch hills and Vallejo's trusted foremen dead in their own workshops and corrals. Only a few half-breed vaqueros and their saggy-breasted whores still hung around. Fremont and the Bear Flaggers had driven off the livestock and stripped the place of anything they could carry. Who cares? thought Galon. He passed through the front gate and sat down against the thick adobe wall. His face was puffed and flushed bluish pink, like the belly of a dead fish. His own breathing made him dizzy. A short distance away he could see his brother and a gang of the half-breeds having a little fun. Beyond them the dry low hills pulled toward the Coast Range like the waves of nausea Galon felt rolling through his body. He closed his eyes and tried to sleep.

Millard was sad that Galon hadn't wanted to join in the new game he was learning. It was a good one. The vaqueros told him it was very old but still popular. It was called *carrero del gallo*.

A chicken was buried up to its neck in the dirt. Then the participants took turns charging the squawking bird at a gallop. The idea was to swing low out of the saddle and pick off the bird's head with one hand in passing. Millard was very good on a horse in spite of his age and came up with the head on his second pass. The half-breeds cheered and Millard felt very proud. He couldn't wait to show Galon. He raced over to his sleeping brother cupping the bug-eyed chicken head in his bloody palm like an egg.

Wake up, Galon, he shouted, shoving his prize in Galon's sleeping face. Look what I won!

Galon woke with a start, eye to eye with the mangled chicken head. Something snapped inside him.

He slapped Millard's hand away from his face and fought for breath. He sucked at the still air but it settled in his mouth like fine dust. He coughed and grabbed for the canteen lying next to him. The water was warm and stale. Millard's smiling babble grated on him like a sandstorm.

Look here, Galon, Millard persisted, shoving the chicken head back under Galon's nose. I done good.

That was it. Galon kicked out at his brother, catching him in the stomach and sending him buckling backward into dust. Galon slid his back slowly up the wall till he was standing and glared at Millard.

Is that what you got for me, Millard, a shit old chicken head? Galon wheezed. I spend my life looking after you and that's what I get when I ain't feeling good. Well, you get the hell away from me. I'm through with it. You ain't never done good. You're on your own and I don't give a fuck.

Millard didn't understand. He stared blankly at his brother and tried to think of what to say. But it was no good, and he was still sitting there in the dust when Galon got on his horse and rode off without him.

Galon headed west, toward the coast. He wanted moisture. He wanted to stand naked in the rain. He wanted the cool relief of mist and fog on his face and in his lungs. For the first time in his life it occurred to him that he might be dying. But imagine how Millard felt.

41/Millard

Poor Millard. Most of the time he was like an empty house: nobody home. His brain sailed back and forth in the space of his head like a phantom trapeze. Dumb habits dominated and he never felt much one way or another, with one obvious exception. He loved his brother.

Millard would have led apes into hell for Galon, and now he was lost, orphaned, like a child told to sit in the corner without the faintest understanding of what he had done wrong. He watched Galon disappear into the brittle golden hills and it occurred to him that the best way to get him back would be to buy him. Galon had always wanted to be rich, so if Millard got a lot of money and could buy Galon whatever he wanted. . . . It is not an unusual line of reasoning even today.

Thus, Millard Burgett, at the age of fifty-nine, set out to make his fortune. He rode east, toward Sutter's Fort and what turned out to be a golden future.

TEN

42/Counsel

Great dark birds sailed huge and aloof on the hot wind above the clusters of blue oak and digger pine that sheltered Counsel's place on the dry, rocky approach to Tejon Pass. Taya and T. D. Jr. rode in, sweating and winded, late in the afternoon.

Everyone around Counsel's had a frontier mind. You could tell by the way each could carry on long and complicated conversations without the aid of another person. The shrewdest spoke of themselves only in the third person, which sounded pretty clever until you spoke to Counsel himself. He was special, a truly superior frontier mind.

In his travels, his bouncing around on the frontier to establish one trading venture after another over twenty-five years, Counsel had come to believe that conversation, talk, was not simply cheap. It was also dangerous. Words were weapons that men used to trick and dominate each other, especially in the trading business. If he let another man impress him as to the worth of, say, a bundle of beaver pelts, it inevitably cost him more money. And if he made the worse mistake of talking about himself, sooner or later it came back to undermine him. Better misunderstood than to let on how your mind works, he had decided. Thus, he never told stories, and more important, he let nothing he heard impress him.

I couldn't care less he had found to be a most useful phrase and over the years he had refined it. First by shortening it to a sly *I couldn't care,* and then, in what he considered a major breakthrough, he had honed it into verbal shorthand with *care nothing.* Eventually, when he reached California, he had hit on the ultimate: *care.*

Yes, it gave him the perfect image. That one simple word used alone, Counsel found, communicated a disdain of disarming power. When Taya and T. D. Jr. showed up that afternoon asking about Buckdown his response was predictable.

Care.

What's this care? Taya wanted to know. But it was no use. Try as she might, she could get nothing more from Counsel. Even T. D. Jr.'s elegant attempts to reason with the trader were met with the same monosyllabic response.

The trappers who witnessed the exchange found it hilarious and volunteered nothing for fear of cutting short what was shaping up to be a real howl. If it had not been for Counsel's wife, Taya and T. D. Jr. might have learned nothing. When she returned from her wood gathering and found Taya almost pleading with her husband, she put an end to the foolishness.

Buckdown is in the North, she said, but he is probably crazy. There are jokes about him.

With that, the trappers figured that the fun was up to them, and proceeded to tell each other Buckdown jokes.

Did you hear that Buckdown won't eat tongue anymore?

No, how come?

He says it ain't clean to eat anything that comes out of an animal's mouth.

Oh, yeah, well then what does he eat?

Eggs.

Taya and T. D. Jr. rode north the next morning, but before they left T. D. Jr. made a daguerreotype, at Taya's request, as a present to thank Counsel's wife. He placed her and her husband in front of the trading post. She sat on a bale of fox pelts; Counsel stood behind her with his rifle. The trappers heckled from the side. Halfway through the exposure, Counsel suddenly wheeled and walked off into the woods. T. D. Jr. knew at once that the plate was ruined, and sure enough, when he developed it there was the woman, clear and sharp in every detail but totally unbalanced in the composition by Counsel's blur fading out of the perspective behind her. T. D. Jr. wondered if Counsel knew Zorro.

43/San Joaquin

Dawn. The sky was pink, pale blue, and shiny. It cupped over the San Joaquin like an inverted abalone shell, tropical and misleading. They were traveling north, straight up the middle of the huge arid valley, through a flatness that stretched in every direction like amnesia. Taya was sullen. Jumpy.

Since leaving Counsel's she had felt herself pushed closer and closer toward the edge of something, something physical, depleting. Yet she wanted to fly toward it, to get to it and see.

She was already mounted, waiting for T. D. Jr. He was seeing to the packhorse, checking his equipment.

Relax, he said. We'll find him.

Yes, she said quickly, if we get moving and don't waste time talking about it.

Her voice was sharp, too sharp for him that early in the morning.

Look, he said, I don't see why you have to be nasty about it. I'm still here, aren't I? And I'm not complaining, am I?

She didn't answer, just dropped her eyes away from him and waited. He walked his horse up beside her and climbed slowly into the saddle. He had hurt her feelings, he thought, and he didn't like to do that. But he was damned if he was going to be badgered into a pace that would exhaust them both and probably kill the horses.

I know how you feel, he told her and was about to explain about the horses when she cut him off.

No you don't.

She spurred her horse into a reckless lope and he didn't catch up with her that day, or that week. In fact, he almost didn't follow her to Sutter's Fort at all. He thought about turning west, straight for the coast and the hell with her. But he didn't, and not because of any promise he had made. No, it was far more complicated than that. In fact, he was never sure himself why he followed her to Sutter's Fort.

44/Rio Fresno

At dusk, Taya pulled up on a bluff and looked northwest. Ash trees quivered in the late breeze along a small river. Two miles farther north, it joined a much larger river, and there, in the crook of that junction, a tribe of Worm Eaters had made a fishing camp.

Purple light thrown off in a glow from the dropping sun lingered in the air, washing the water birds in a florescent pastel. When Taya looked due west, she noticed the rolling dust of a band of mounted men. They were headed toward the fishing camp. Taya had two choices: warn the Worm Eaters about the night riders headed for them, or forget it and ride on about her own business. She spurred her pony toward the river.

By this time there were about a hundred thousand Worm Eaters left in California, about half as many as that Majorcan-born soldier of God Junipero Serra had found in the bushes when he had shown up to save them seventy or so years earlier. And the fact that there were, even in this year of our Lord 1846, only a few hundred Californios, Mexicans, Europeans, and gringos loose in the land made the Worm Eater weeding-out process seem all the more successful. Hell, it hadn't been easy, especially in light of the Worm Eater's timid manner. The young ones were sometimes tough to find.

Riding into the fishing camp Taya wasted no time. As the braver of the Worm Eaters snuck out from behind their tule huts to stare at her, Taya jumped from her pony and drew the sign for bad trouble in the dirt.

As she rode on, her shortening shadow only confirmed what she knew the moment she had seen the dust to the west. A bad moon was rising.

45 / Gente de Razón

Only mitten-heads voiced occasional sympathy for the plight of the Worm Eaters. Aside from slavery, simple and direct homicide was the most popular method of dealing with them. And, indeed, as old T. D. Slant was often heard to say, it was difficult to spend a weekend drunk or sober without encountering at least one of their pathetic corpses.

But consider poor T. D. Jr., who encountered three hundred of them on the banks of the Fresno River where it flows into the San Joaquin. Strange, he thought, as he walked through the carnage in the moonlight, so few of them are women. This was the wrong meat for his mind to chew on and he knew it, but nothing could be done. He wasn't about to admit to himself that he half expected to find Taya's lithe young body dead and cold among the corpses.

She had probably ridden right through. He hoped so.

ELEVEN

46/Galon

Crabbed and wasted came Galon Burgett to Fort Ross. Twittering sarcastically back at alarmed birds and hawking heavy plugs of yellow phlegm into the foxtails, he scuffed his way around the perimeter of the abandoned fort. Multicolored fungi drove silently between cracks in the log wall like wedges.

Galon was feeling better. He searched through the various sheds and lean-tos for a new home. There was one large cabin that might do. Two rooms, actually, with smooth plank floors and a scatter of furniture that Galon eyed with satisfaction. But he couldn't have everything. The place reeked of fish oil.

Pinecones, Galon thought, perhaps pinecones placed in the corners would get rid of the scaly odor hanging in the tight air. And he could make his bed of boughs and redwood shavings and the fire would help and then—hold everything! There in the far corner of the smaller room he saw a bed, a nest really, of fresh pine cuttings.

Someone or something was recently holed up in the old czarist outpost. Galon drew his pistol and turned cautiously back toward the larger room. Suddenly the front door slammed. Galon fired at the noise, splintering a half-inch hole through the door at eye level. He charged forward, reloading, to take cunning advantage of the smoking new peephole, but it was a wasted squint. There was nothing new out there, or so it seemed.

He stepped out into the windless dusk. Something was fishy. An old sensation stalked along his nerves, a tingle he had felt many times before. He tasted his own spittle turning to cotton on his tongue. He was not alone, he could feel it. He was being watched.

47/Shaboom

Shaboom Watanabe, lost son of Yedo and a stranger all these years in this strange land, squinted through the thorny bushes overgrowing the front gate. At last a man alone had come to him. Shaboom studied the man, remembering. He ground his teeth. He cursed the wretchedness of his curious mind, the mad hunger that so long ago had made him turn his back on the fine points of feudal honor and sail out of Yedo Bay craving travel and knowledge.

He had hung around Deshima, listening to Dutch

sailors paint wide visions of a world beyond, and when he got the chance he had shipped out. And then shipwrecked, and the Russians and the insults and insidious oblivion of this stupid coast on the edge of the world. He had tried to escape once and had learned his lesson, an expensive lesson that had resigned him to stay put.

How long ago, he wondered, had he snuck down to the beach at night and stolen that kayak? It was a treacherous memory, but not without its moral, the lesson he knew only too well. He had paddled south, gobbling raw fish for strength, nosing ashore each night to sleep in sandy caves. He had hoped to find refuge and passage home in the bay of San Francisco, but floated past its narrow gate in a rainy morning fog. He kept going. Thirteen days out of Fort Ross found him bobbing, exhausted, off Monterey. The next thing he knew a ferocious squall was blowing him further south and within an hour the wind was surfing his delicate craft straight for the rocks of Point Pinos.

Fished out dripping and disoriented from the churning shallows by some fun-loving Californios, Shaboom had been asked but one question.

You got any money?

When he shook his head, trying to collect his wits, they tied him facedown over a horse and galloped into Monterey. And then, before he could explain himself, they had thrown him into a large wooden cage where he spent the next three months. Yes, he shuddered to think about it. The Californios had started a zoo around him.

On display between a three-legged horse and a

gila monster that slept all the time, Shaboom had gone predictably mad in a matter of days and become a great crowd pleaser. He shrieked and threw his own excrement.

The exact circumstances surrounding his escape remain a mystery, but under the headline CRAZED JAP AT LARGE, the *California American* had suggested that perhaps the Russians were involved. Was there not a Russian ship in the harbor, the paper argued, and had not some of its officers been observed conversing in front of the fugitive? And had it not looked like he understood whatever the hell they were saying? The paper's editor, T. D. Slant, knew good copy when he saw it and his news judgment told him to ignore the fact that he had seen someone he knew very well tinkering with the cage on the very night of the Jap's escape.

The paper's innuendos naturally resulted in a call for action, but an intense search of the Russian vessel had turned up nothing but sea otter pelts. Shaboom, meanwhile, had been cutting a zigzag trail north, determined on an elegant suicide to show the Russians. Just to show them.

But he had found Fort Ross deserted. The Russians were all gone, having sold out to Sutter, who had come with his Worm Eaters and carted everything movable back to his fort while the Russians sailed away with a small chest of gold nuggets that Sutter had told them came from Mexico. Shaboom had stood alone in front of the fort and decided to wait. It was his fort now and he would command it one day at a time, waiting for a visitor and a chance to get even.

Since then Shaboom had dug out the necessities of his increasingly moribund existence like a common Worm Eater. He caught fish with his hands. He dug roots on the ridge and gathered kelp-heavy mussels from the rocky tide pools. Only his spiritual training saved him from fading into the thick wilderness like an extinct animal.

Twice each day he stared west in meditation and managed somehow to find the ordered vacancy of the gardens of Kyoto in the fog that rolled in below him like a curtain closing over the ocean.

Now he contemplated his visitor, his guest. The man was obviously not a Russian or even a Californio. No matter, he would have to do.

TWELVE

48/Sutter

Gathered around the gate at Sutter's Fort, Millard Burgett found an assortment of Californio layabouts bemoaning the arrival of the Mormons. Willing to work harder for less money, the Mormons, it seems, were grabbing all the good jobs.

But Millard was not discouraged. He was determined to make his fortune for Galon. He rode inside looking for Sutter, the man himself.

John Augustus Sutter would probably have wound up very rich were it not for two egregious dings in his generous and otherwise progressive character: (1) he gave advice in crowds and (2) he had a tendency to play both ends against the middle. Thus, he was eternally overrun by the weak and indecisive while the people he should have been able to count on didn't trust him. Old T. D. Slant was given to referring to Sutter, in print, as a toadying sycophant. Millard Burgett, on the other hand, came to admire and esteem him. Such were the whim-whams of Sutter's public image as he sat in his office adding a long column of figures.

Outside he heard the evening bell clang and put down his pen. It was his favorite time of day, feeding time for the Worm Eaters. He smiled to himself and walked outside.

Running along the fort's eastern wall was a shallow wooden trough, one hundred feet long. Sutter noted with satisfaction that very little of the warm gruel poured into it by the heavy-ankled women who worked in the cookhouse was spilling to the dust. Waste not want not, he always said. He walked the length of the trough, stopping only once to dab a thick finger into the soft mixture of beans and corn to measure the consistency. He didn't want it too thick.

Presently, the first wave of Worm Eaters came pouring through the side gate. Close to two hundred of them crowded into long lines behind a rope that had been stretched waist-high, parallel to the trough. All eyes were on Sutter. He backed out of the way, and with a sweep of his arm signaled that the rope be dropped to the ground.

Feed yourselves, he said, smiling benevolently, and reached in his vest pocket for his pipe.

Millard had never seen anything like it. The Worm Eaters surged to the trough and began scooping its contents into their mouths with cupped hands. And already a second wave was forming at the gate.

Close to an hour passed before the last Worm

Eaters had jogged in from the most distant fields to gobble down payment for a day's labor. Forty-nine huge caldrons of the bean-and-corn mixture had been poured like slurry into the trough, and through it all Sutter had quietly smoked his pipe.

Millard was overcome with respect. When Sutter set out on the rest of his evening rounds, Millard followed at what he hoped was a respectful distance, gathering nerve to approach the great pioneer. Sutter toured his storerooms, checking the number of hides and candles and sacks of wheat. Millard dogged him with growing admiration. Finally, when Sutter was on his way to his own supper in his private dining quarters, Millard tugged at his sleeve.

What do you want? Sutter demanded gruffly.

A job, Millard told him. I want to work for you.

So does everybody. What can you do?

Millard was stumped. He hadn't worked it out that far and could only stand there toeing silently at the ground as Sutter walked away from him.

49/Honest Work

The times were ripe for frenzy and, knowing what he knew, Sutter found himself in a very busy and rather delicate position. Acting as go-between for the various factions of Californios, Americans, Mexicans, and assorted other interests in this joke of a revolution, he cursed the fact that it had come before he was ready and he stalled for time. Like most people who find themselves cast in the role of middleman, Sutter had much bigger things in mind for himself.

In only eight years he had built his New Helvetia into a medieval barony, outsmarting an endless string of Indian raiders, Russian interlopers, French plotters, English trappers, and American adventurers, not to mention his Mexican hosts and Californio neighbors. Now he faced the biggest test, and it all depended on keeping one secret until he was ready for what he knew would follow its disclosure like a storm.

Late that night, Sutter sat at his writing desk. A tiny fire smoldered in the corner of the stone fireplace. It was too hot for a fire, but it kept him alert, lest he forget the humiliation of a shotgun wedding and bankruptcy in Switzerland, the land of fireplaces. Never again, he mused, looking into the flames. Rich and powerful, he called himself captain now, and wore the uniform of an officer in the French Guard which he had picked up somewhere. He would win out in the end if he could just keep his balance. He took his pen in hand and began to list his problems. It was a list of names.

There was Fremont, of course. . . . That mercenary glory hound was mucking up everything with his swagger and entirely too much ambition. Fremont had even locked up Vallejo right here in New Helvetia, telling Sutter to keep the dignified Californio as a guest for a while, or else.

Valejo, yes . . . he was another problem. The man had controlled too much to simply give up. He read too much and he had powerful friends, Larkin for example.

Larkin, hmmm. . . . Hard to understand but definitely sneaky, that Larkin, with his secret land deals and contracts. He was no friend of Fremont, yet they seemed somehow to be working toward the same end. But then Larkin had warned him about Brannan.

Brannan, well. . . . It was too soon to tell about Brannan, but if it was true, as he had heard, that Brannan had hired that son-of-a-bitch Slant and given him a newspaper to run, then something had to be done.

Slant, shit. . . . That crazy propagandist had been a pain in the ass from the beginning with all his talk about the dangers of concentrated power and his dirty connections.

Dirty connections, of course . . . all those self-serving revolutionaries browsing at the edges of everything, crisscrossing the countryside from one nefarious rendezvous to the next clandestine deal. And some of them were probably working for him, even as they worked against him.

So . . . Sutter read over his list and decided to make deals with everybody he could, just in case. He'd show them. He wadded the piece of paper and tossed it into the fire.

There was a knock at the door. Sutter waited until his list darkened into charcoal before answering. It was Joaquin Peach, one of his new labor bosses.

I hired another man, a funny little American, Peach told him.

Sutter frowned.

Don't worry, Peach insisted, he's too old and stupid to cause any trouble.

He's an American. What's his name? Sutter asked.

Burgett, and he's got a good gun. I can use him to guard the Worm Eaters cutting wood on the river.

Very well, but keep him away from me. I don't like Americans.

50/Go Away Closer

Taya missed running into Millard at Sutter's Fort by less than a day. As it was she ran into Joaquin Peach. She rode through the front gate and was surprised to see the roto walking around giving orders. When he saw her, he bowed with a flourish.

I have moved on to bigger things, he said.

She could see that, but was in no mood to listen to how. Early that morning, she had come across a band of Worm Eaters. They had been shouting at the sun, talking to it as if it were listening, encouraging it to continue its rise as if it might not. Then suddenly a bunch of Sutter's men came and herded them off. That the Worm Eaters could be so straightforward all the time, and so vulnerable, had struck Taya somehow. They had such simple ideas, worshipping everything they saw in the hope that more would appear. And then lying down in front of any stranger to be stepped on like the dirt itself. It made her uneasy. She didn't want to think about it anymore, and Peach's success obviously had something to do with it. He was carrying a whip.

How's it going? he wanted to know.

Where's Zorro? she shot back.

The question threw him. Why, he didn't have to feel guilty for leaving the old hero, but that's how she had made him feel. On purpose, he imagined. He'd show her:

Where's your husband?

Husband? The roto was getting out of hand. She brushed past him into the main office and took a room for the night. Husband? T. D. Jr.?

The next morning, Taya ran into Peach at the corral. He was probably waiting for her.

I'll bet you don't even have a husband, he said with a smile. I'll bet you're pretty loose too.

He was trying to be funny, trying to flirt a little, but it was definitely the wrong approach. Taya slugged him in the arm and turned abruptly, just in time to see T. D. Jr. come riding through the gate. No big surprise really, she had expected him to catch up sooner or later. She glanced back at Peach, who was not smiling, and ran to meet T. D. Jr.

T. D. Jr. was pleased. He had followed her, less than a day behind, in spite of himself, and if she was glad to see him, then it was worth it. He hoped she needed help.

Hi.

Hi.

How sweet, Peach said, and smirked at T. D. Jr.

Ignore him, Taya said. He has bad manners.

Bad manners! Peach was outraged. If there's anybody here with bad manners, he said to T. D. Jr., anybody who forgets who their friends are, it's your wife.

Wife? T. D. Jr. said he didn't have a wife.

Oh, I get it, Peach said. He whistled through his teeth and started swiveling his hips at Taya like an aroused dog. Boys will be boys.

T. D. Jr. jumped him from the saddle and a fistfight ensued. Taya acted like she wasn't interested. Maybe she wasn't. She walked away from the two of them grappling in the dust and saw to getting fresh horses. When T. D. Jr. and Peach realized that she wasn't watching them, their enthusiasm wilted and the fight was over. The crowd that had gathered jeered at them for not acting like men.

Taya was waiting outside the gate. When T. D. Jr. found her she snapped at him.

I can take care of myself, she said.

Then go ahead.

But he didn't want her to leave. It was a game they had begun to play. Call it *go away closer*.

They both gave in. It was determined that if they had not found her father by the time it snowed in the mountains, she would accompany T. D. Jr. back to Yerba Buena, where they would both reconsider everything. That settled, they rode away from Sutter's Fort and made an early camp that afternoon on the American River.

51/American River

The sky was thin, weatherless. Taya had some questions. She was not sure what she was up against in the puzzles of men.

She heard the fervid ticking of grasshoppers in the

tall grass that stretched back from their camp on the lush river bank. The scratchy breathing of lizards and toads hung in the thick summer dusk like pagan tapestries. When T. D. Jr. told her he'd be right back and walked leisurely upstream, she waited a moment and then followed him. She tracked him silently, a short distance off to his right. He stopped in a grove of ferns, faced a deadfall, and unbuttoned his trousers. She moved closer.

Casually, he drew out his penis and took aim at a line of red ants moving along the rotting wood. His yellow stream squirted out and splattered the insects, tracing their supply line with a smooth stain that began at once to disappear. With a flick of his wrist he was done. As the last drops fell at his feet, he turned his head and there she was, studying him.

Offering no explanation, no apology, nothing, she reached down and took hold of his cock. It felt cold and weightless in her palm, like a small dead bird. He just stood there, unable to move, as she examined him. She stretched him out, noting the suppleness and the tender pink mushroom of a head. On an impulse she suddenly squeezed with all her strength and was surprised that he didn't flinch. She began kneading and soon felt him begin to grow and harden. It seemed to her that he was filling with hot sand. She looked up into his face and saw him trembling.

I . . . I . . . he stammmered. You. . . .

She released her grip and walked back to camp. He joined her presently and tried to make small talk. He asked her mundane questions about the weather. She could tell he was embarrassed and ignored him.

She had to think. The river slid past her, hurrying to sneak through the delta and on into the San Francisco Bay. She had no way of knowing, of course, that one of the men she was after would make a discovery of his own at that very spot less than a week later, a discovery that would twist all their lives again. Even old T. D.'s in far-off Yerba Buena.

52/Brannan

Dogs barked. Roosters crowed. Early birds lost in a grey sky sailed over the stainless bay of San Francisco searching for the mud flats.

Damnable fog!

Old T. D. Slant tumbled irritably into the morning, the furry residue of last night's brandy hanging in his throat like spider webs. He felt his life moving ahead of him, like the town itself, growing just a bit too fast. And no wonder, he had taken up with Brannan, that landjobbing Mormon from Maine.

Already Brannan had a suburb of adobes squatting among the sand hills at the beach. He had his people slapping up two flour mills on Clay Street with the lumber he had others milling down the peninsula and had his eye on some of the action at Sutter's Fort. Plus, he was initiating publication of a weekly newsletter to be called the *California Star*. That's where old T. D. Slant came in. Consider Slant a consulting editor.

There was much to be done and Brannan had con-

fessed to Slant his need for someone with hard edi-
torial experience, someone who knew the territory,
a nuts-and-bolts, meat-and-potatoes, ball-and-cap,
jack-and-hammer sort of fellow to help him whack
out his grandstand ideas. The Mormon saw California as a fine country, an ecology favored with a
bountiful nature by the Lord himself. A good place
for good people. Yet he also perceived waste, both
physical and moral, cysting up like so many carbuncles on the fair face of paradise. Something had to be
done and, as president of the Associated Immigrants
for God, Brannan felt the lance of responsibility
heavy in his hands. The decadent Californios and
their swarthy Spanish ancestors had accomplished
practically nothing in the way of good works, and
the Worm Eaters were, of course, beneath consideration. It was time for nature's more worthy children,
he told Slant, time for them to step in and set grade
for the road to prosperity. And his newspaper would
be like a clean wind, blowing away the old fogs of
sloth and ignorance, scattering the seeds of development across the land. Brannan heard California
singing.

Old T. D. Slant was amused. What a colossal joke.
But then what is a joke to a man with a jaded life?

53 / Foothills

T. D. Jr. looked at the peaks of the Sierra Nevada in
the distance and thought they were spectacular. He

raved to Taya about the majestic qualities of the lay-
ered light he saw shining down through the passes.
And what scale!

But getting there proved tricky. As they rode farther up into the foothills, his wonder at what he saw
in the distance gave way to the insidious frustrations
of where he actually was. The bleary flatness of the
giant valley that fell away behind them looked comfortable in comparison. The steepening hills were
thick with brittle growth unimagined in the East.
Ticks dropped down his collar. And worst of all, a
full day of sweaty travel seemed to gain them nothing. Trails disappeared in dusty box ravines and the
cresting of one ridge merely called up the need to
crest another. There was no end to it, like chasing
the horizon.

His only pleasure came in the evenings. He would
remove his shirt and sit with his back to the fire
while Taya searched him for ticks. Her fingers
skimmed over his clear skin like tiny water birds. He
felt them in an intricate and gentle tatoo across his
shoulders and down his spine. Then the twisting
pinch, and she would lean close around him with
one of the parasites on display like a peppercorn ooz-
ing blood between her slender fingers.

Since the American River, a certain tension had
been tightening between them, and he ached for her
now, for her smooth legs and perfect hands. He
imagined tracing them with his tongue, taking all of
her delicate parts between his lips and. . . .

Late at night, cock in hand, he would stare at her
across the dying fire and shut out all else. Gone, the
clouds flying past the moon and the wind purling

through sumac and oak. Gone, the hard ground beneath him and the beasts ranging about in the dark. Gone, everything except his image of her, pacing his climax like a string of mules winding up into some far-off pass. Then wet spurts, and he would rise up in an arch before falling back on his blankets to moan himself to sleep.

A light sleeper, Taya would sometimes be awakened by his muffled howling and ask him what was up. He would explain earnestly that because he was an artist he had the dreams of an artist. And such dreams were incomplete without certain guttural punctuation. The muse demanded it, he told her, and he had no control anyway.

He assumed she understood that he was just being polite, and hoped that she was flattered by such exquisite and complicated longings. But she considered his dreams presumptous and icky. When he tried to explain what he was feeling with subtle hints and innuendos, she yawned.

It was not that she didn't have healthy appetites of her own, or that she didn't like him. She liked him fine and even felt a certain tingle when she looked at him sometimes. But she had decided that certain things were impossible.

Then one day, when they had almost cleared the foothills, she asked him about his dreams. They had stopped earlier than usual and were looking back down over the way they had come. She wanted to know if his dreams were always the same.

No, he told her. Except they are always, uh, inspiring.

She didn't say anything. He thought maybe he had

misunderstood her question. Perhaps it wasn't a question at all, an invitation maybe.

I dream about beautiful things, he said, hoping it was what she wanted to hear.

She still didn't say anything. He felt her silence tightening around him as if he had made some terrible mistake. He decided to take a chance. He asked her about her dreams, what they were made of, what she saw in them.

Dead animals, she said.

Buckdown would have been proud.

THIRTEEN

54/Buckalo

Who was to say that Buckdown was crazy? Certainly none in his herd. He schooled them in inconsistency, teaching them never to move in any discernible pattern. He emphasized milling about, like so many shag balls blowing on the wind. And when trouble came they must scatter, he insisted, gallop off like smithereens. It would drive the white hunters nuts and make the Indians even more respectful.

Some were slow to understand, but he was patient, touching them constantly, assuring them, loving on them. Eventually he even took some of the slower learners as wives, figuring that his seeds, packed as they were with savvy, might improve the line.

Buckdown explained later that couplings were rather awkward at first, but by the spring of 1846 there were a number of little buckaloes roaming with the herd. If Buckdown is to be believed, it is not unreasonable to speculate that these results of his snortings into the bovine life force had something to do with the eventual long march into Canada that saved what was left of the herd many years later. It is impossible to know for sure.

Anyway, Buckdown lived with the buffalo and tried to forget. Occasionally he would leave his herd to seek out His Own Ghost. The strange Indian was always glad to see him. They would smoke a little tolache together and consider various aspects of the mythic content. Buckdown aspired to join the ranks of the Animal People, a pantheon with which His Own Ghost was sociable. But the sly albino was not about to forfeit his connections with a hasty or un-distinguished recommendation and was somewhat standoffish whenever Buckdown broached the sub-ject.

Your motives are pure, His Own Ghost would tell him, but I'm afraid there are certain weaknesses in your background. All that animal murder in your youth, you know.

But Buckdown would not be daunted, and his de-termination never failed to touch the shaman and make him feel proud, like a warrior when a daughter asks why she, too, cannot steal horses. So although His Own Ghost knew that he could not in good con-science encourage Buckdown, he cheated a little and did not discourage him either.

When it was time to say goodby, His Own Ghost always presented Buckdown with a new supply of

his potent little buttons and one of his favorite dou-
ble-edged cantos: *Go your own way and you will get
what you deserve.*

His Own Ghost knew that the Animal People were
always watching. They were very sneaky.

55/Animal People

To and from his rendezvous with His Own Ghost,
Buckdown routinely sabotaged whatever works of
man he came across. Former colleagues, making their
rounds to collect the soft pelts that made such fine
hats and coats for the sissies back east, found their
traps prematurely sprung and their bait buried. Such
men were, of course, too singleminded to suspect
one of their own kind of such bizarre and unnatural
subversion. They figured it was the arrogant red man
again, axing, out of ignorance and envy, at the roots
of an obviously superior wilderness technology. Incidents occurred.

As for the Indians, whenever they found a fish
dam mysteriously busted or watched a herd of antelope veer suddenly away from a carefully conceived
ambush, they usually cartooned the event into their
oral history as the Great Spirit having a little fun at
their expense. Occasionally, however, if Buckdown's
mischief was a shade too obvious, a philosophic
brave might build a fire and proceed to dead-color
the sky with smoke signals suggesting (generally
with a rather heavy-handed irony) that the Animal

People were at it again. Buckdown could read their smoky semaphores and was encouraged by such flattering speculation, but back with the herd he was never known to brag like he had in his book.

FOURTEEN

56/The Edge of History

Brass-colored light bounced off the water. Not hot
yet, but a stickiness hung in the early morning air
like a promise. Gnats were hatching in the eddies
downriver, and from somewhere back up the bank
in the trees, Millard heard the mumblings of naked
men marching to work. It was usually his job to
watch them, keep an eye out that they didn't damage
the logging hardware or run off to their mud caves
before quitting time. But not today. It was Millard's
day off and their singsong moaning seemed as am-
biguous and remote as whatever he was going to do
next.

Take the day off, Joaquin Peach had told him. You
know, relax. Think about bigger things.

Millard was stumped. What to do? He wished
Galon were with him. Galon would know. Galon. . . .

Millard certainly missed his brother. And it was all so confusing. What had happened, that is. His memory scattered back on him like a loose pattern of buckshot through a forest of petrified regrets, pinging here and there off how sorry he was. But since he had no idea why Galon didn't like him anymore, Millard's recall suddenly jumped to the good times, the good old days on the Rosebud, buffalo runs through the Tetons, frisky trades at Counsel's first place on the Wind River, high glee toots in Taos. Whoopee, he remembered their song:

> *Oh mountain men, how great are we,*
> *We cannot stand for trifles.*
> *We hang our balls on canyon walls*
> *And shoot 'em down with rifles.*

Yeah, that old T. D. Slant got what he deserved for getting it all wrong and making Galon mad. Maybe Galon would like him again if he got the literature fixed for him. Maybe if he got Buckdown. . . . Anyway:

> *We fuck our wives with bowie knives*
> *And feed on bears and pickles.*
> *We wipe our ass on broken glass*
> *And laugh because it tickles.*

In high spirits now, Millard set off with new resolve to do good for Galon, to do good on his day off, and to do good in his work for Sutter. Galon would see.

So Millard Burgett went wading up the shallows of the American River looking for helgramites and wound up staring over the edge of history.

57/Eureka

When his eyes caught the curious yellow sparkle, he pondered not at all. It was instinct. Gathering himself like a puma about to leap some dark chasm, Millard plunged his arm elbow-deep in the clear water and grabbed. His gnarled fingers closed around a gold nugget the size of a dog's eye, and his crusty palm began to tingle with anticipation.

He scrambled up the riverbank and into the tall grass. He crouched like a fetus. He turned the soft metal over and over in his trembling hands. He popped it into his mouth and bit down, tasting a sweet pain on his rotting teeth. Millard was a fool no doubt, but this was definitely the real thing. Eureka!

But now what? He peeked out through the reeds, his eyes wide and cryptic. Across the river, a family of valley elk, timid except for antlers, dipped velvet noses into the current, drinking. And so was Millard, but he was quenching a different kind of thirst. His tongue worked new saliva around the nugget bulging in his cheek like an acorn.

Events would shape themselves from here on out. Cause and effect were finally in play again. A brand new game was about to open and the trump turned out to be sneaky and vicious enough to rival the wine-drinking, virgin-seducing catechisms of the missions in their heyday. Millard, of course, had no idea. The possibilities were beyond him as he raced off to show Sutter how good he had done.

58/The King of California

Let's keep this our little secret.

Sutter weighed the nuggest in his hand and winked at Millard for emphasis. Lord, this was all he needed, a secret partnership with a geriatric half-wit who didn't have sense enough to wink back. Sutter needed more time. And there was still so much to be done, so many arrangements to make. The situation was getting much too volatile. Schemers were lurking everywhere. That jingoist Brannan was waiting for him in his inner office at that very moment.

Millard kept watching him, smiling like an adopted puppy. Sutter wanted to grab him by the throat and squeeze, wring every last yelp of breath from his stupid life. But he didn't. Instead, he produced a key which he kept hidden next to his skin and moved to a long cedar chest, heavily inlaid with cherry and walnut, that waited in one corner of the room like a coffin. Make that a sarcophagus.

Close your eyes, Sutter told Millard and proceeded to open the chest and rummage through what sounded to Millard like metal plates. When Sutter finally instructed him to open his eyes, Millard saw before him a mandolin with little lambs depicted in romp about the sound box.

Go on, take it, Sutter told him.

The mandolin made Millard very happy; it was smooth, it was clean, and it made noise. Millard plucked and fondled it in front of the fire while Sutter laid out the conditions of what he called their limited partnership. How could Millard possibly guess that Sutter had already made plans to relegate the official discovery to one James Marshall, a man of ordinary intelligence and little style. So Millard just grinned.

Sutter, of course, smiled back at him and, in the end, put his hand gently on Millard's ragged shoulder. He led Millard to the door and even opened it for him. Remember, Sutter whispered, just between you and me.

With Millard gone, Sutter sent for Joaquin Peach and began pacing in a small circle around his writing desk. Things could be worse, he told himself. And if he couldn't handle some half-wit, then he didn't deserve to become king.

59/Millard's Brain

Serious and crucial talk between Sutter and Brannan over the next two days. Both obviously had things to hide. Millard, meanwhile, hurried back to the scene of his wonderful discovery, unaware that he was being followed.

He splashed into the shallows, collecting an assortment of nuggets, and then took up a position from which he could keep a sharp watch on the claim as Sutter had instructed. He sat on the riverbank, dangling his toes in the water and twanging away on his mandolin.

Millard had been what was called marked in the brain at birth. And most men he met, Sutter for example, found his reason sadly lacking. Millard never understood insults or the dangers of a bad reputation, and it was almost impossible to hurt his feelings. He had never been in love. Few things ever moved him one way or another. It was not understood back then that a person like Millard might appear stupid for any number of reasons, or that in rare cases the brain produces its own morphinelike substance that acts as a natural pain-killer. Millard's was such a case, and it should be pointed out that so far he had lived his life not so much stupid as stupefied.

Then, *bang!*

The rifle ball that lodged behind his ear with a thud as he sat there on the bank of the American River changed everything. It hurt, of course, and stunned Millard for a moment, but it did not kill him. Rather it dammed the reservoir of renegade enzymes that had been drowning his synapses for so many years, and he began to get smart. He began to think.

He knew at once who was responsible for the attempt on his life and a lot of others things as well. Punch lines of wit and reason fell through his head like confetti. In a flash he was on his horse and away, riding with thoughtful purpose toward the coast, making plans.

FIFTEEN

60/Other Changes

It wasn't just old Millard's mind that was changing, no siree, cabron! Things were up all over. Take T. D. Jr., por exemplo. His clear young artistic eyes were doing a fandango with a fortified mix of Sierra Nevada landscape, and the muckworms of greed were hatching in his heart. A man's first view of his promised land inevitably hits him with the fear of being somehow cheated out of it, and that's exactly what was happening to T. D. Jr.

He was standing on a flat white slice of granite overhang, staring down maybe three thousand feet on the most beauteous slash of wilderness he'd ever seen. His mind hollered at him. Look at that lake, and the way those two silver rivers slide into it all smooth and heavy like milk, or bloodlines maybe. It was spectacular. Delicate feathers of mist floated up the canyons that spread out from the basin like the spokes of a wheel, and the sunlight was shooting in and out of it all like a hail of arrows. Tiny rainbows everywhere and it was all so quiet and weighty. And natural?

All T. D. Jr. knew was that he wanted it. No, needed it. All of it, the ponderosa pine and the golden trout and the air itself. He'd build a stone house, a castle. And sire strong sons who would sit with him at a heavy redwood table and together they would . . . well, for one thing, they'd keep everybody else the hell out of what was his. Naw. It wasn't all that bad. The sons would be more than brutes and he himself would run the show with a lot more style than all those rough-handed partriarchs dreaming that same old dream of isolated empire. *His* kingdom would be refined, tempered with the inquisitive sensibilities of science and art. One son a botanist, another a poet, another a geographer, another a student of archeology; and his daughters would be blessed with the natural grace that makes pianists and lacemakers superb wing shots. Each morning he would kiss Taya's fingers one by one and life would proceed as an elegant seminar into the natural order of things. Even the NO TRESPASSING signs would be done with taste.

He kicked a small rock off the ledge and walked back up to the narrow ridge where Taya was resting with the horses. He looked at her and saw his future as a tableau, a tapestry of fine threads. If he could just set up the loom in time, the weave would take care of itself. He felt nervous with luck.

It's steep, he told Taya, pulling his map from the

saddle pouch. But there's a pass on the left and there's a lake. It's perfect.

Perfect?

Yeah, hurry.

Hurry indeed. She couldn't figure him. Ever since the American River he'd been playing a sucker to his own whims. Maybe she shouldn't have grabbed him. She turned and looked west, where they had been. A line of mountain sheep stared up at her from the switchback below. She stared back until shadows thrown from above skimmed over the sheep and they spooked. Condors, she figured, but when she looked up the sky was empty.

Wait up, she yelled, turning to follow T.D. Jr., who was now carelessly breaking trail a quarter of a mile ahead of her.

But he didn't wait, and it was hours before she came up on him. He was on the last steep rise above the lake, studying his map. He looked up, smiling, and waved his arm in an arch.

It's not even on the map, he said.

There are lots of maps, she told him.

And she was right. In fact, there were far more accurate charts of the area, some even delineating their own history; and it wouldn't be long before T.D. Jr. would have to face a few facts about who owned what. And not just in terms of real estate.

61/Slant Lake

The autumn dusk came nesting down on the lake like a great soft animal. Pine shadows dissolved in the rich purple twilight. Small clean waves licked quietly at small stones on the narrow beach. Taya sat watching the horizon move toward her over the water, pushed by the darkening sky.

They had been three days at the lake. At first she had welcomed the rest, admitting finally that she was tired. The fall days were warm and dry and the creeks were ice cold and wonderful for drinking. She had rested and stitched at their tattered clothes while T. D. Jr. roamed about the lake carving his name in trees.

She tossed a pebble into the water. She was rested now, strong again, anxious. Funny how the body gives and takes in its own rhythms, teasing the will. And stranger yet how spirits or pieces of spirits are always trying to crosscut those same time streams of the body renewing itself. Taya wanted to move on once again. She had to, even if it meant dragging her body like a bone at the end of a rope, plowing beneath the soil on the Sierra edge of California.

T. D. Jr. came out of the trees and sat down beside her on the narrow beach. He picked up a flat rock and skipped it across the water.

You like it here? he asked.

It's all right, she said. She did not look at him.

I like it here, he said, sweeping his eyes over the darkening lake. I could live here. I'd like to live here.

When?

The question surprised him, embarrassed him somehow, drained at his enthusiasm, made him feel silly. Sometime, he told her. Just sometime.

There will be snow here soon, she said. Her voice was flat.

So that was it. She was worried about giving up. Maybe even afraid that he. . . . His mind raced. Didn't she know? He had known the moment he had seen her again at Sutter's Fort, and now more than then. It had to do with his destiny. You bet. He rested his arm over her shoulders. It was the very first time he had done this, but he did it with confidence. She could tell.

Don't worry, he whispered to her. We'll find him.

And for the first time in all the months that they had been together, she leaned on him.

As the darkness closed in around them, he felt her relax into sleep. He looked up at the stars, an infinite scatter of twinkles winking down at him. Something definitely tricky going on up there. He had no god, but Lord, he thought, don't mess with me now. He bent closer to Taya, asleep against him, and was about to venture a kiss when they had a visitor.

62/The Immigrant's Guide

It was Lansford Hastings, a definite face card in California's fresh deck of knavery. Yes, an author, lawyer, and character assassin, Hastings was destined to distinguish himself in a high propaganda capacity with the Confederate States of America. But first, he had fortunes to seek in California. He rode boldly into the shrinking light of their campfire.

Children, Hastings announced, if you're heading down into California, I do hope you've a copy of my indispensable guidebook to see that you get your rightful jump at fortune in that shining land.

Taya drifted back into sleep. Hastings said he was riding straight through, bound for the Humboldt Sink, to intercept as many frontier amateurs as he could find arguing in their wagon trains as to the relative opportunities waiting for them in California as opposed to Oregon. He figured to turn them south via a shortcut he had invented for his book and eventually herd them into the Central Valley, where arrangements had been made with Sutter.

The plan called for Hastings to lay out a town to be christened either Sutterville or Hastingsberg, depending on the outcome of further negotiations between the two men. He had accomplished a dog-walk survey for the development in less than a week, complete with piles of dirt clods indicating future intersections of importance. Sutter, meanwhile, had dispatched as many Worm Eaters as he could spare to the American River to cut wood. Sutter planned to sell the lumber to his future neighbors at a substantial profit, and Hastings had part of that action as well. Everything seemed to be falling into place. All Hastings needed now was a couple hundred immigrants to seed the place with their small-scale dreams.

He banged T. D. Jr.'s ear tirelessly for hours. And when he finally left, he told T. D. Jr. to look him up if he was ever interested in a corner lot in a good neighborhood.

Thus, T. D. Jr. heard about the future, and Taya woke at dawn to find him in a grumbling depression. He was like the kid who finally determines to jump off the roof of the barn only to discover that some other kid has already done it.

Hastings said he's going to bring hundreds of wagons through here, T. D. Jr. said. He says he might even stake out a rest stop here, and then a town. Right here.

He'll never make it, Taya said.

And they rode on into days that became routine. He woke depressed each morning and seldom spoke to her. She would build a small fire and he would brew coffee. They would drink it watching the fire die and then head north once again. He didn't know what he wanted anymore. He began to doubt his own sanity. She told him that it went with the territory.

SIXTEEN

63/Haiku and Seek

Galon Burgett was heading out of his mind. The sun was in and out all day, playing peek-a-boo with him from behind dusty white clouds. And Shaboom was dabbling in the same game. He popped from shadow to sunlight and back, erasing himself, giving Galon just the faintest image to wander after through the otherwise deserted outpost of Fort Ross.

Light to dark, sunlight into shade, yin-yang and the edge in the middle; it was insidious. Each time Galon crossed the line he went blind for at least a second, and it was then that Shaboom hooted haikus at him:

> *Dead belly crying*
> *Full of fish for you*
> *California*

Just noise to Galon, like clipped animal snorts flying on the wind, but there was something in the pitch, the rhythm maybe, that made him shiver. He felt his own death. Was it sneaking up on him?

The games people play. . . .

64/Vallejo

One hundred tricky miles inland, Vallejo was dreaming of Worm Eaters. He saw long lines of them, stacks of his hides balanced on their heads. They were trotting naked over unfenced land, through hills swaying with wild mustard, toward the embarcadero.

Sutter shook him awake.

It's me, Captain Sutter.

Vallejo opened his eyes and nodded. He recognized Sutter right off. The bastard.

Look, I'm sorry to have to keep you locked up here at my fort, Sutter said. You know it's all Fremont's idea. Were it up to me. . . .

Vallejo nodded again. He was good at nodding. Indeed, he had nodded his way into a position of great authority on the northern frontier. When as a handsome Californio he had nodded to the Spanish padres and dealt sternly with their runaway Worm Eaters, he had been well rewarded. Then he had nodded to a string of Mexican governors and was rewarded again. At the age of twenty-seven he had held the title of Military Commander and Director of Colonization. His civil and military power blanketed the north. All he had to do was nod and things happened for him. His wealth of land and Worm Eaters multiplied. Then, suddenly, the Americans, and try as he might to nod along with whatever they had in mind, his empire began to fall apart. Now he was middle-aged and in jail. Imagine his chagrin.

Sutter winked at him.

You and I have always been honest with each other, Sutter lied. Right?

Vallejo nodded to the lie and waited for Sutter to get to the point.

We have always been in harmony as to our own interests and the interests of this fair land, Sutter continued. In fact, the only reason you are detained here now is that *you* convinced me that our best interests lay in supporting the Americans. Is it my fault that they don't trust you as much as they trust me?

Again Vallejo nodded, but now he was thinking that Sutter and the Americans deserved each other. The only American to be trusted was Larkin, and he knew that Larkin thought Sutter was a toe-counting nincompoop. And his old friend Slant had told him all about the broader American view of Sutter.

Glad you agree with me, Sutter said. But I didn't wake you up to talk about that. The way I see it, you and I still have the same interests: protecting our holdings. It is true that yours have been somewhat, shall we say, trimmed? But I think you will have to agree that the last thing either of us needs is an influx of undesirable citizens. I am speaking of capitalistic engineers, get-rich-quick speculators, the kind of men who have traditionally been drawn to certain economic rumors. I fear such possibilities exist here, and I am asking you to help me keep the lid on.

Sutter paused, then slipped his secret into the conversation like a fishhook.

I have heard there might be gold around here, his whispered.

Sutter searched Vallejo's face for something given away in surprise, a *meaningful* reaction that would help him plan his next move, a clue. Something, anything! But the Californio didn't even nod. The two men stared at each other like sentries.

Of course, Vallejo finally said sarcastically, all kinds of it, just lying around. El Dorado, don't you know. We Californios have jokes about it.

Ha, ha, ha. . . .

Sutter relaxed and produced a paper from Larkin for Vallejo to sign if he wanted to get out of jail. It transferred the ownership of a number of acres on the eastern lip of San Francisco Bay. Vallejo nodded and signed.

65/Sacks Without Seams

Vallejo was only half kidding. Seeds of the sun, as the Worm Eaters called the flakes of the baleful yellow metal, were not uncommon. Californio women of all classes wore little golden pebbles as ear drops, and most Californio men who cared for jewelry had a ring or two fashioned out of the stuff. And there was a joke that if you wanted to take the trouble to look for it, gold was easy enough to find. It was just that it took too much trouble. The Californios, you see, were repulsed by any labor that could not be accomplished on horseback. Thus there was no fishing and even less scratching around in the dirt looking for gold. A chunk found lying around was naturally picked up and pocketed, but nobody every really went looking.

Unfortunately for Sutter, however, California was filling up with men who didn't mind doing a little looking for whatever they heard might be free. Millard Burgett, for example, and he wasn't the only one.

There were others peeking into the golden future. A few nuggets and small quantities of dust were popping up in unlikely hands. Stashing began. A certain roto made plans to pass the word to Valpariso when the time was right. It was obvious that there was at least some gold in California. The question was, how much? And more important, would there be enough to go around? But there had been no substantial discovery, at least as far as anybody knew. Gold became a sensitive subject inside slapstick rumors. A man had to appear well informed on the matter or risk not being let in on something big, if something big ever happened. A man had to bluff.

And there were ways of telling if a man had more than a wishful-thinking understanding of the possibilities. Take the regulars at Cargo West, for example. In sizing anyone up these days they looked for a sack without seams. More than just handy containers for carrying around one's future gold dust without fear of losing any, the little bags became symbols of those in the know.

It had all started when the rotos introduced the traditional dust purse of Chilean prospectors, leakless little sacks fashioned from the scrota of butchered rams. The stylish and masculine accessory was an immediate hit. Everybody who was anybody just had to have one. Especially old T. D. Slant. He was naturally skeptical about the rumors of vast amounts of gold, but he saw in the soft little sacks a chance to redefine his masculinity, and to make up for a certain vacancy that no doubt preoccupied him. Early on, he purchased a faded pink sack from Joaquin Peach, who happened to be in Yerba Buena to confer with the loudmouthed Brannan.

No sooner had Peach returned to Sutter's Fort than old T. D. started referring to himself as Money Balls, claiming that his purse was in fact fashioned from his own scrotum. Circumstantially, he had no trouble proving it.

He didn't intend to offend sensibilities, at least he said he didn't. No, he simply wanted to establish some dignity for himself and others in his condition by boldly illustrating one of his oldest postulates: that a sack of gold could be just as important to a man as a hard-on. He even wrote himself up in Brannan's newspaper, cautioning emulators to use only the sharpest of blades and plugging a new brandy label he had recently invested in as the best sterilizing agent.

Word of Money Balls reverberated over California like a high-pitched screech, piercing the eardrums of the avaricious like a white-hot needle, searing, merciless. Californios were shocked and sickened. Even the mercenary rotos were outraged and disgusted by this perversion of their original concept. To the Americans, however, especially the Mormons, it was

an intriguing idea, especially if one substituted another man's hard-on. Thus, it became a widespread
and high-status practice to employ the scrotum of a
dead man as a purse for small change, and Josiah
Sewey naturally felt a certain smugness when word
of the new fad reached him.

I already got mine, he said demurely, and liberated
old T. D. Slant's stiff and crusty sack from the confusion of scalps and animal teeth in his medicine kit.
Only his ignorance of the fact that Slant and Money
Balls were one and the same kept him from affecting
unbearable pretensions in his new and lucrative
career.

66/As Time Goes By

If they had thought about it, Taya and T. D. Jr. would
have called themselves lost. The terrain was strange
enough, some kind of high volcanic plateau cut with
bubbling rivers and seep holes; but it was the wild-
life that had first made them concentrate on each
other instead of where they were. Horned larks
soared above mule deer the size of their horses. Per-
petually agitated porcupines with deep-red quills
chased around near the rivers, snapping butterflies
out of the air. Spotted eels pulled loons beneath the
surface of eddies. Owls, some the size of dogs, others
the size of spiders, flew in straight lines between
yucca and hemlock trees. Some rodents also flew.

They quit making camps when they woke one
dawn to find themselves surrounded by a perfect cir-

cle of pointed black rocks. The rocks looked as if they had been there forever and appeared to have been tooled. Very spooky, even for Taya. So they rode on, sleeping nights in their saddles, concentrating on each other for courage. Maybe they were falling in love, and maybe that love was so perfect that the rest of the world could only look vicious, mutated against the natural course of such a love. But probably not.

More likely that love had to wait on nature, and Taya and T. D. Jr. were like ships, not so much passing in the night as heading for the same hijack port. Certain destinations can make everything on the way look real scary.

67/Taya and T. D. Jr.

What a trip. Finally out of that spooky landscape of the previous week, Taya insisted on leading. No more weird routes for her. T. D. Jr. agreed completely and fell in behind her. Conversation between them relaxed. They felt casual, as if they had known each other for years and could tell each other crazy things.

I was afraid to tell you, T. D. Jr. said, but I thought I saw an ape back there.

Was he wearing a Mexican army uniform?

How did you know?

I saw him too.

SEVENTEEN

68/Buckdown

In spite of advancing age, Francis Buckdown was a handsome figure of a man. He wore his thick black hair in a fat greasy braid that fell below his waist. At the end of the braid he hung various ornaments, depending on his mood. Feathers sometimes, sometimes bits of carved bone, and when he was feeling especially festive, a small tin bell that jingled when he ran. Sporting the bell, he was seldom mistaken for anyone else. This was how they found him.

There he was, belly-deep in cattails and wild onions, in a high valley outlined vaguely on T. D. Jr.'s map as Big Meadow. His herd stretched up the meadow behind him, grazing demurely. Buckdown looked the picture of bovine pride as he stood there testing the wind, alert so that nothing should sneak up.

That man has obviously lost his mind, T. D. Jr. observed, focusing in on Buckdown in the distance.

He and Taya passed the small telescope back and forth. They consulted the picture on the book cover. It was Buckdown all right. Gently nudging her pony, Taya rode slowly out into the meadow. T. D. Jr. drew his pistol and followed.

Buckdown's reaction upon seeing Melting-Snow-Of-Winter-That-Chases-Despair for the first time in almost sixteen years was predictable. He didn't recognize her. No remembered picks of things past twanged on the strings of his heart. Indeed, no gut strings tugged anywhere in his laced-up emotions as he moved cautiously toward the intruders. He was just doing his duty as he saw it, all very straightforward, resigned. There would be no animal murder this day in the meadow, not if he could help it. He circled them several times, crouching low and then bounding closer in quick starts. They pulled up and waited.

Powwow time, Buckdown decided, and advanced to face them. He cocked his head, wondering at this woman with the hard distant eyes and this young man with the nervous horse and drawn pistol.

And they were facing him, this old man gone clearly crazy. And clearly dangerous as well, as T. D. Jr. found out when Buckdown swatted the pistol out of his hand. Next, a long thick face-to-face silence, some kind of ritual stare-down. Taya knew it was up to her.

Father?

Now hold on!

Buckdown took three giant steps backward and

waited for the punch line. He scanned the ridges for a sign. He frowned like a sour old fool and farted indignantly.

Very rude of him, but how would you have felt in Buckdown's moccasins? Better walk a mile in them before you criticize. You lost your wife too many sunsets ago to remember. You are seventy-one years old and not getting any prettier. You have been to the end of the earth and have seen a beach covered with animal blood. And, for almost a decade, you have been living with a herd of mountain buffalo, gobbling peyote.

Men came after you, Taya said. But they got old T. D. and they got me.

Buckdown blinked. The realization of exactly what was happening didn't hit him until Taya handed him the book with his picture on the cover. Then it hit like a bucket of icy water, very sobering. His eyes literally rattled in their sockets. He was obviously coming back from somewhere very far away. Taya read it in his face, surprise and anguish, like a horse falling off a cliff.

Buckdown held up the book and traced a berry-stained finger over old T. D.'s name on the cover.

Did he send you? Did your father send you?

Now it was Taya's turn off the cliff.

Buckdown wanted to explain, but it was all so long ago and so very complicated. He made T. D. Jr. wait in the meadow and led Taya to a thick stand of aspen where he got the story of what happened in Monterey. Time for him to consider responsibilities once again. The weather was changing, and a gradual darkening thickened in Buckdown's head to match what was happening in the sky. Taya became the time stream. Buckdown saw what he had to do just as clearly as he heard the first thunder cracking toward him over the ridges.

69/Free Gold

The Burgetts would have been easy enough to find if only Buckdown had remembered to read the weather. The storm blowing in from the west was a trail of sorts, readable. He could have backtracked it over ridges marked by lightning fires, could have followed it straight to the coast where it was renewing itself over and over in a juggle of tumbling static pressures just off Fort Ross.

The old fort was a regular weather sink, a funnel actually, that sucked at the Pacific and blew waves of hard rain east through a natural spout in the Coast Range. And although Galon Burgett appreciated the moisture, he couldn't get used to certain other factors, natural and otherwise, that trespassed on his convalescense. All that noise on the wind, for example, and all the strange signs. This night, this storm, found him again unable to sleep for more than minutes as a stretch.

Shaboom, meanwhile, sat in his cave contemplating the clumsy storm walking around in the black sky, and it occurred to him that in the end he would become like the thunder. But not yet, and he prayed in his own mysterious way that the lightning would not take its flashy game of electric tag to Galon and pronounce him *it* before Shaboom was finished with his own game. Shaboom had his own zoo now. It was his turn.

Day after day Shaboom played on Galon's failing health, his dwindling ability to do for himself, with the psychological swat of unseen hissings in the darkness. In the predawn fog, Shaboom would pad silently to Galon's door with a day's ration of acorns and clams. He would arrange the food in a shrinelike little pile and then use an eclectic collection of dead animal paws—beaver, fox, goose, frog, etc.—to track the signs of much animal travel to and from the offering. He was careful, of course, to cover his own tracks.

Weak and disoriented, Galon had no idea where the real world had gone. The food kept him alive and he welcomed it, but at the same time he was terrified by the possibilities. Where was it coming from? He would sniff tentatively at the eerie mix of animal tracks, convinced that he was being fattened up. Very spooky. And then there were those taunting, singsong shrieks. . . .

The moon broke through the storm. Shaboom peeked around the entrance to his cave and . . . what's this? Coming up the path to the fort, he caught a shadow on the run. Too many fatherless shadows in this wilderness to speculate, so he was up quickly and on the move, stalking his way carefully down into the fort for a closer look.

Galon sat propped against the wall on his bed of redwood cuttings. He picked at his fingers. He searched over the lines in his palms. Like all men, he wanted to live forever, sure, but not like this, not tormented by some devious pack of one-footed devils. Better, perhaps, to beat them to the end. He reached for his rifle and began to lick the muzzle. Now what? To be or not to be? . . . Finger on the trigger now, Galon brooded deeper and deeper into the choice until suddenly, bursting in on him, came brother Millard.

Greetings from El Dorado, brother!

Millard rushed to Galon's side, spilling a sack of bright nuggets and yellow dust on the bed. Galon's jaw dropped. His rifle fell across his lap. He grabbed Millard's arm.

Where'd you rob it?

I didn't rob it, Galon. It's free.

Free gold? Galon shook his head.

Millard's explanation made Galon dizzy. It wasn't just what he said, it was how he said it. Could this be his dumb brother making leaps of reason, articulating subtle implications, actually explaining something to him? . . .

Observing the scene through a crack in the door, Shaboom fixed at once upon the free gold. For the first time in many years he thought about escape. His mind leaped forward, picturing a first-class sea voyage on one of the sleek traders he had seen every year or so running south off his coast toward San Francisco. All to be bought and paid for with the shiny metal Galon was now fingering. Wasting no time, Shaboom took a deep breath and knocked sharply, very businesslike, on the rotting door.

Needless to say, the Burgett brothers were startled.

They exchanged amazed shrugs, then suspicious nods, and turned narrow eyes on the door. Galon cocked his rifle. Millard drew his knife.

Come ahead.

In walked Shaboom, his moon face beaming. He bowed back and forth, from one brother to the other. Galon didn't know whether to shoot or shit apples. Millard too was speechless. Shaboom pointed at Galon.

You're dying.

What's it to you?

It's unnecessary, said Shaboom and proceeded to explain that he knew a place where it was acceptable, common even, for a man to live forever. It was far away from this wretched coast, however, and reaching it required not only a long and expensive journey, but the services of an expert guide as well. Someone like himself, also expensive.

What kind of a scam is this?

Shaboom elaborated, flipping out the details of paradise as reasonable alternatives to being enfolded by the very wall of death that Galon felt backed against. Soon, Galon was hooked. He felt his age passing into a new scale of measurement. Forever. He turned, smiling sheepishly, to his brother.

Well, Millard, how about it?

Financing will not be a problem.

70/Demographics

Riding into Yerba Buena, Vallejo wondered where they all came from, all these wild-eyed men with

their faces twitching in the same ironic smile. Moun-
tebanks to a man, he speculated, like Fremont and
those Bear Flaggers. It was unnerving. Didn't they
have a country of their own? Born in hell most of
them, probably.

Not quite. Old T. D. Slant had done a survey for
the paper and his records show that the citizenry of
Yerba Buena, not counting Mormons or Worm
Eaters, gave their birthplaces as follows:

United States—121	New Holland—1
California—81	New Zealand—1
Mexico—51	Australia—3
Texas—24	Peru—8
Chile—21	Poland—1
England—12	Russia—1
France—3	Sandwich Islands—5
Germany—7	Sweden—2
Ireland—7	West Indies—3
Scotland—2	Africa—1
Switzerland—3	At sea—4
Denmark—1	Could not recall—1
Malta—1	

Old T. D. Slant had gathered the data as part of a
study to project the demographic possibilities of
Brannan's paper. To aid the Mormon on his advertising calls, Slant had also determined that 173 of them
could both read and write, 113 could read but not
write, and 89 could do neither. But everyone was
upwardly mobile.

Vallejo would no doubt have found Slant's find-
ings interesting. He was himself an avid reader and
personally owned the only substantial library in California. His passion for books had caused him
threats of excommunication from the mother church
on three occasions. The good padres were contin-

ually catching him with dirty books. Only his shrewdly worded letters to the pope saved him in each case from eternal damnation.

His friendship with Slant had grown out of their mutual interest in the printed word. They had discussed its power often at great length in the old days. Slant also supplied Vallejo with books. He ordered them through Larkin. It was tricky because Slant and Vallejo had to meet each shipment in a small boat and smuggle the contraband ashore before the ship dropped anchor, and had to submit, under one of the very laws Vallejo was supposed to enforce, to a moral inspection of its cargo by the prying padres.

The only good news that Vallejo had received during his incarceration at Sutter's Fort was a letter from Slant telling him that his old book-running friend was sick of literature, life itself for that matter, and was giving him his library for the sake of old times. Vallejo didn't know what to make of the letter, but he certainly wanted the books. Slant had some real treasures, Balzac's racy *Droll Stories,* for example. So as soon as he had bought his way free of Sutter, Vallejo had come straight to Yerba Buena to find out if Slant was on the level.

He found Slant pounding on the bar at Cargo West, telling the elegant Greek barman that all of California south of Santa Barbara should be left to the greaser Mexicans and good riddance. The Greek insisted that the south coast had the only climate in the territory fit to cradle a civilization.

Civilization indeed!

Anyway, Slant might not have made good his promise of the books had not the first thing out of

Vallejo's mouth been an inquiry after Taya. Slant hadn't heard her name in months, and the sudden mention catapulted him once again into a guilty fit of remorse and worry. It was not that he had forgotten about her. No, it was just that he had been doing well emotionally as Money Balls, somehow managing to keep his guilt private. And now. . . .

Slant pushed his library on Vallejo like a mindless exorcist trying to purge himself of all the devilish stories that men write down. That *he* had written down, caused. He ranted that he was done with such things, for good this time. His own vices, his interest in Mormon sex, had seduced him back into the stinking word racket, but never again!

I quit, he yelled down the bar at Brannan.

Vallejo was amazed at his friend's peculiar behavior but was too polite to ask questions. He just nodded and had some Worm Eaters load the books into a wagon, and the two old friends got on with the business of drinking out the night in silence.

When Vallejo got home to Sonoma he wrote Slant a thank you note which included this bit of business advice: Beware of Sutter. He plans to usurp your port. He now has the land I was planning to use.

71/Relative Futures

T. D. Jr. had it all worked out in his head. He might have appeared silly on occasion over that last few months but perhaps only in comparison to Taya. After all, he was a young man and therefore given to certain moods and inconsistencies. He was no fool, but he was also in love.

As he saw it, the perfect future looked like this: Taya realizes his gentle strength. She falls delicately in love with him. They make wild, youthful love at every opportunity. She forgets about revenge. They marry. She becomes the wife of a great artist. And he would also like to have that lake he liked so much, if it's not too much trouble.

Buckdown was wise to T. D. Jr.'s intentions, had been since they met, but he didn't know how to handle the situation. You see, Buckdown also knew Taya's secret, another thing he knew right off.

One day they made an early camp along some bright unnamed stream and Buckdown went fishing. Actually, he poised himself on the bank with Taya's saddle gun and waited to blast the first trout that happened to slide across his aim. T. D. Jr. found this strange enough to sit close by and attempt a fast study in his sketchbook as had become his custom since running low on everything necessary to make daguerreotypes.

Taya had walked upstream. It was assumed that she had gone to bathe in a large smooth eddy they had passed shortly before stopping.

T. D. Jr. finished the sketch just as Buckdown decided that it was a shade too early for the fish to come feeding to the surface. He set down the rifle and tried to peek at T. D. Jr.'s sketch. T. D. Jr. didn't mind. He wanted to talk, maybe brag a little. When Buckdown said he liked the sketch, T. D. Jr. decided to test the murkier waters where art meets life.

I plan to marry Taya, you know.

I know. What about the baby?

Baby?

The one she's carrying around with her. The one that sure as hell ain't yours.

This was the real-life factor that T. D. Jr. had refused to think about since he had figured out what had happened to her. He hated it.

Shit, he said.

See for yourself, Buckdown said.

T. D. Jr. had to, of course, so he followed Buckdown, sneaking upstream like an indignant colt made to follow an old mule. Taya wasn't far. They slid up a wooded little rise on their bellies and peeked down at her. She was naked, thigh deep in the still water, and sure enough. . . .

If there is music for the way T. D. Jr. felt, it should be played on a silver flute with large agates of soft quartz scraping against each other in the background.

EIGHTEEN

72/Perfect Worm Eaters

Yerba Buena was careening into a strange and violent period by the time the child started kicking in Taya's womb. Almost overnight, street life became rash, dangerous. Rain, like sheets of mucus, drenched the ground into sticky, boot-sucking mud. In the cold twilight, tentative men with coats pulled up around their faces scurried back and forth doing business. Everything stayed open late. Assaults were common.

Old T. D. Money Balls Slant would spot a Worm Eater lurking ineptly around the pockets of the waterfront and be unable to resist sending him on a fetch. Over one especially cold and foggy weekend, two particular Worm Eaters had successfully delivered into Slant's hands a gull egg, a wild strawberry, an abalone shell suitable for use as an ashtray, and six sets of elegant fish eyes swimming in a tiny glass jar.

These Worm Eaters seldom spoke, and if they ever slept no one knew where. Yet their energy seemed boundless. They were said to know their place in life. They asked nothing in return and were willing to fetch for anyone except other Worm Eaters, although they occasionally fetched one of them. Their fetches for Money Balls were always the most eclectic and they loved them, but they also seemed to enjoy more mundane assignments. A toothpick for Brannan, say, or a container of grease for Wild Emma. And although not everyone rewarded them for their efforts, they always appeared animated and cheerful, as if wagging invisible tails.

Perfect Worm Eaters!

73/Sewey

Josiah Sewey took careful aim and blew one of those giant birds out of the sky. The Worm Eaters worshipped them, so Sewey couldn't resist. In fact, they were his favorite targets for sport shooting, and sport shooting was his favorite diversion now that he was an established businessman. After splitting up with the Burgett brothers, Sewey had followed a brand-new career in an industry that had been pioneered in northern California by Hippolyte Weed. The business was slaving.

Over the years, Weed had developed an aggressive yet subtle word-of-mouth marketing network. By

1846 he was selling comely little Worm Eaters from what were considered the cleaner northern bands not only to Wild Emma through the Cargo West connection, but also to bureaucrats in Mexico and various ranchos up and down the coast. He had even founded a small settlement close to the Oregon border which he named after himself and used as a base of operations.

He employed several half-breeds and Mexicans as assistants and was becoming a wealthy man. Then, shortly after hiring Josiah Sewey, whom he had known from the old days on the Platt, Hippolyte Weed mysteriously disappeared.

Some said he had drowned in the Klamath River. Others said the Worm Eaters got him. Sewey said it was a shame either way.

And guess who took over the business?

74 / Ass Kicking

Always curious, the perfumes in California's meadows, but Sewey caught a stranger scent, one that had no business in these parts. He was sitting on his horse watching an assistant repair one of his holding pens when suddenly he smelled buffalo. At first he thought it was just the musk of the two pretty little Worm Eaters inside the pen, but no, it was definitely buffalo. Then suddenly a familiar voice:

Long time no see, Josiah, you mother-fucker.

It was Buckdown, riding out into the open. Taya

and T. D. Jr. stayed in the woods and started making noise. The idea was to make Sewey think there was half an army waiting for him in the trees.

I hear you been wanting to kick my ass, Josiah. Is that a fact?

The assistant went for his gun and Buckdown put a bullet through his eye. Another dead Mexican.

I don't want to kick nobody's ass, Sewey said.

Sewey was thinking that Buckdown could probably still kick his ass, as he had done on several previous occasions, and he wanted very much to get it lost before he got it kicked again. Or worse.

Buckdown rode closer and said: Well in that case, Josiah, you shit-sucker, would you happen to know where I might find Galon and the half-wit? I hear they've been wanting to kick my ass and I sure do want to get it kicked. You sure you don't want to kick it for me?

Ah, come on, Sewey said, I got a nice little business going here. I don't care about kicking ass anymore.

Well then, Josiah, how about if I just beat you to death?

Sewey realized he had no choice. Eat it raw, he yelled, and spurred his horse. He was desperate. He was also very lucky, for at that exact moment Taya was squeezing the trigger of her saddle gun with his desperate old face balanced in the sight. As it was, she almost killed Buckdown.

When Sewey jumped his horse, Buckdown jumped his own in pursuit, crossing directly into the line of Taya's fire. Thus, the day did not work out the way any of them had planned. Buckdown got his ear shot off and Sewey got away.

And things were about to get even worse.

75/Walla Walla

The Worm Eaters that Sewey left in the holding pen turned out not to be Worm Eaters at all. They were Walla Walla, children of that unusually belligerent tribe that hung around the California edge of the Oregon Territory. Some among them, most notably the sons of old Chief Yellow Serpent, had been educated at a missionary school in the Willamette Valley, where they had acquired a ragged proficiency in the English language and a taste for white-man baiting.

The Walla Walla band that swooped out of the trees and captured Taya, Buckdown, and T.D. Jr. right after Sewey got away had three things on their collective pagan mind. They wanted their women and children back, especially the virgins. They wanted to do a bit of stealing. And, if the opportunity presented itself, they wanted to repair a little justice for the death of one of Yellow Serpent's sons, a young prince named Leicer, who had been killed the year before on the first Walla Walla expedition to Sutter's Fort.

It seems that Leicer had become involved in an argument with a Kentuckian named Grahm, who was at the fort to help Sutter design a distillery. Leicer was known as a great rascal even among his own people, but it remains unclear whether or not Grahm had been justified in blowing his head off. Leicer's buddies certainly hadn't thought so. They had hurriedly set off for home, claiming that they would return to make everybody sorry.

Now they were on their way back, and at the head of the party was old Yellow Serpent himself. It was his inclination to summarily croak the prisoners like toads underfoot and be done with them, but luckily Buckdown had an old friend traveling with the raiding party. It was that old keeper of the secret buckskins and stimulating medicinal flora, His Own Ghost. He pointed at Buckdown.

He's not one of the Animal People, His Own Ghost told the chief, but he's not bad.

The shaman went on to explain that Yellow Serpent's interests would be better served by using the captives as hostages than as torture toys. He went so far as to claim that they were valuable. Reluctantly, Yellow Serpent agreed to wait and see, and no sooner had His Own Ghost saved Buckdown's life then he realized that he would have to do it again. Buckdown was bleeding to death.

Remember tolache, that smoking weed that had changed Buckdown's life some years before? Well, His Own Ghost once again had some handy. The shaman fired up a pipe, handed it to Buckdown, and started cooking up some buffalo fat. Yellow Serpent's band had been rich in buffalo fat since their exceptional good luck traveling through Big Meadow—where the beasts had seemed confused, leaderless.

When the fat began to boil, His Own Ghost stirred the tolache into it, forming a heavy paste the color of pus. Next, he packed it into the flat hole where Buckdown's ear had been and poked a flower into it. He also covered Buckdown's remaining ear with the stuff.

Maybe, if you have shaped up, the tolache will help you, His Own Ghost told Buckdown. But remember it might kill you, and if it does it's not my fault.

Apparently the tolache thought that Buckdown was shaping up. Although he never grew a new ear, the wound was completely healed by the time the Walla Walla unloaded him.

76/Traded

The appearance of the Walla Walla at the northern tip of the San Joaquin panicked the few settlers in the region, and they fled south to Sutter's Fort, spreading exaggerated reports as to the strength of the war party, predicting massacres and bloodbaths.

Sutter didn't like it. The only men who enjoyed Indian fighting were all on their way south with Fremont to fight the Californios at Cahuenga. If the reports were even half true he would be hard pressed to defend his holdings. The spineless settlers would be worthless if the Walla Walla were as crazed as he had heard. Maybe he could buy them off.

It was raining three days later when Yellow Serpent and his band came hooting up to the front gate. Sutter met them with a box of beads, but Yellow Serpent wasn't interested in trinkets. He signaled for his prisoners to be brought forward and made Sutter an offer he couldn't refuse.

I'll give you the crazy one, the pregnant one, and the other one for twenty rifles and as many barrels of whisky, the chief said. And I won't burn your fort and kill everybody.

Done, Sutter said.

Greatly relieved, he led the chief to his new still. Toasts were in order and pretty soon Sutter and Yellow Serpent were acting like old drinking pals. By morning, the silver-tongued Sutter had persuaded the chief to enlist his band in the struggle against the greasers, promising that the Walla Walla would be compensated handsomely for services rendered and could raise whatever hell they wanted with any and all Mexicans and Californios without retribution.

Done, Yellow Serpent said.

The Walla Walla Irregulars rode south to join Fremont that afternoon, but without the spiritual guidance of His Own Ghost, who had mysteriously disappeared during the drinking.

NINETEEN

77/Galon

Another windy night at Fort Ross. Galon woke coughing from a sweaty sleep and staggered out into the darkness. But rather than prowling silently off to die like an old cat, he picked his way to Shaboom's cave. He was anxious to talk again about immortality, to listen as Shaboom explained about the high mountains north of Yedo where large white dogs rolled playfully among miniature trees. A place where men who had the courage of no regrets could slide gracefully into forever. And the best part: how there was gambling and sex and fierce hawks to watch in combat in the sky. And even grass-stuffed pandas for target practice. Oh boy!

Galon felt better. If he could just get there, fitting in would be a snap. He'd samurai it up with the best of them; all he wanted was a chance. He smiled, tentatively, across the flickering fire at Shaboom.

Shadows jumped in spasms across the rough walls of the cave. The cave was a womb, a stone womb, vibrating in the skittish light. Galon gathered himself into the fetus crouch, anticipating his future, waiting to be spurted into a new life, born again.

Tell me more, Galon whispered. Tell me about the hawks again, and the women.

Shaboom giggled and took it from the top, ad-libbing flurries of metaphors. Paradise was a safe jungle. Immortality, a peacock plume to wear in your hat, a rhapsody of shimmering colors. Yours for a sack of gold.

78/Main Chance

The Main Chance as understood by Shaboom was in five simple steps:

1. The healthy brother gathers the free gold.
2. Down to the bay of San Francisco.
3. First-class passage across the sea.
4. Home.
5. Every man for himself.

So far it was working out. The healthy one kept returning every few days with new nuggets for the growing stash, while the sick one fell deeper and deeper into the fancy net of promises Shaboom strung together each night. And even the logistics appeared to be falling into place.

The last time the healthy one came he had brought a newspaper. The sick one read it aloud. On page three, surrounded by an account of a band of Walla Wallas (whatever they were) joining a politician named Fremont, there was a very promising advertisement.

TRADING MISSION TO EXOTIC FAR EAST

Messers. Thomas O. Larkin and Samual Brannan announce the charter of the sturdy bark *Eagle* for the purpose of a capitalistic venture with the spice-and-silk kingdoms of the Orient. Consignment space available. Contact Larkin or Brannan c/o Cargo West, Yerba Buena.

That's where we been talking about, the sick one exclaimed. Ain't it?

Shaboom nodded and watched, smiling as the two brothers danced a little jog. The sick one sang and babbled to the healthy one about how jealous somebody named Sewey would be if he found out that they were going to live forever.

79/Sewey

Where the hell was Sewey?

He knew where he was. Where the hell was Wild Emma is what he wanted to know. He sensed a double cross. Here he was at the agreed upon rendezvous with the promised string of comely Worm Eaters and not a sign of his contact. He hadn't expected Wild Emma to show up in person, but she had promised to send a launch with someone in her stead if she couldn't make it.

Sewey scuffed up and down the cove, muttering to himself about trying to do business with a woman. He told his Worm Eaters to find themselves something to eat and climbed up the cliff again for a long look south. Not a sign. He cursed the curve of the earth for shortening his view. Below him his Worm Eaters waded in the shallow surf, digging up clams with their toes. What was he supposed to do, swim them to Yerba Buena? And what about the money?

He'd been waiting almost a week. Maybe Wild Emma was dead. She sure as hell was going to be if this was a double cross. He pulled out his pistol and fired into the sky. The Worm Eaters looked up from their clam digging and he waved them up the cliff. He'd be damned if he was going to wait around this shit hole of a rendezvous any longer. He tied the Worm Eaters single file behind his horse and took off at a trot for Yerba Buena. Their feet didn't matter; you don't screw with your feet.

80/Taya

Meanwhile, at Sutter's Fort, Taya decided that the world could shove it. She had dealt with dread a long time and now she was mad. She terrified the Worm Eaters, striding among them, insisting on secret abortive herbs. Buckdown, and even Sutter, found it impossible to meet her stare. She told T. D. Jr. to grow up.

TWENTY

81/Horizon Lines

Pregnant women always spook people so, make them so uneasy, make them ask so many questions. Especially old men.

Boy or girl?

Who's the lucky daddy?

And behind Taya's back when she ignored them: I wonder what got into her, ha, ha, ha. Cream's fattening, ha, ha, ha. And seriously: women aren't no good once they get knocked up; you can't fuck 'em anymore and they get uppity.

She wanted out. Oh, how she wanted out.

Do something, she told T. D. Jr.

Fast, she told Buckdown.

Anything, she told herself.

But all three of them were still the property of Sutter. Technically speaking, he owned them. Not that he had any use for them as far as he could see, it was just that nothing in this world was free. Their freedom had cost him. They were bought and paid for. He pointed this out and asked what they thought would be fair.

He had to be kidding.

Hardly, Sutter told them, let's make a deal.

He finally settled for a series of daguerreotypes T. D. Jr. executed over the next week. Sutter chose the subject matter and dominated the tone of each composition with an astounding lack of taste. The man definitely had a vision, a self-concept with flying colors. Poor T. D. Jr. bristled under each of the theatrical little playlets Sutter insisted he record: Sutter in a rabbit-pelt cape, standing in front of the fireplace in his hot, airless office; Sutter at the gate of his fort, surrounded by kneeling Worm Eaters; Sutter gesturing toward the distant mountains with a ceremonial sabre; Sutter naked, contemplating an apple, rejecting it.

T. D. Jr. was especially bitter about having to use the last of his plates on such an obviously bloated ego when the winter sky in the west was carving hard and elegant edges on the horizon.

What difference does it make? Taya asked him. He could see as much high art as he wanted. So what? When she looked she saw vanishing points closing beyond the world like the tips of a scissors.

82/No See'ums

Swarms of life waited for them in the delta, like atmospheres of invisible teeth. Traveling on foot now, leading the one mangy pack mule that Buckdown had managed to steal from Sutter, they were at the mercy of even the most evanescent of creatures. But such life forms are not indiscriminate. They ignored Taya, Buckdown, and even the mule, and went straight for T. D. Jr. They hit him like a storm, a horde, a flying army of insect mongrels ravaging his sweet body like a decadent civilization. And he couldn't see them, couldn't even feel their bites.

Half a day into the marsh country that seeps like a soggy fringe north and east from the Bay of San Francisco, T. D. Jr. was a swollen caricature of his former self. He was a balloon boy, his skin puffed tight, bloated pink. He itched all over. His fingers and toes throbbed like fat little sausages sizzling on a dry griddle. He fainted.

They dragged him onto the driest spot available. While Taya covered T. D. Jr. with blankets, Buckdown built a fire.

T. D. Jr. came to, convinced he was dying, being looted of all his strength and will, he was sure of it. He opened his eyes, blinking watery forget-me-not pleas toward heaven, and there was Taya.

She was sad and caring, he thought, but then all of a sudden she was fanning smoke at him with his own hat. And Buckdown, he was smearing T. D. Jr.'s face with wet, sticky mud.

No See'ums, Buckdown explained. Act like they don't exist.

T. D. Jr. tried, but it was like trying to ignore the hiccups. From then on they were lucky to make five miles a day. They had to stop constantly to repack T. D. Jr. with fresh mud and resmoke him against the merciless No See'ums.

Awkward and irritating days raked like fingernails on slate into damp, almost sleepless nights.

Taya had water-snake nightmares, or dreamed that she was sitting on a rock in the middle of a draining lake. The child sucked inside her. T. D. Jr. fished at her for sympathy. Buckdown tried to comfort her. She hated all three of them.

It was getting pretty hysterical there among the dripping tules and the misleading sloughs, when who should overtake them but Lansford Hastings, riding poker-faced with new deals and the latest news from Sutter's Fort.

83/The Immigrant's Guide II

Another brand-new city, Hastings told them, I'm founding another one. Who needs a corner lot?

He jumped gingerly from his horse and unrolled a map, babbling about prime locations and growth potentials. Taya noticed that Hastings had lost weight. Indeed, he explained, in a survival bout with the wilderness.

T. D. Jr. blinked his swollen eyes at Hastings and started pawing deliriously at the map: what happened to my lake?

Funny you should ask, Hastings said. The fools might have to winter there. It's not my fault though, can't blame me that they didn't keep up. Can't blame me that the snow flew a little early. God knows what they'll find to eat, the lame amateurs. But that's Sutter's worry now. If he wants them he can go and get them, the worthless butt-draggers. I played it smart, traded the miserable lot of them and that minor subdivision we had set up for them back to Sutter; Sutterville he's calling it now. A stinking climate there anyway, too hot. Leave it to the Worm Eaters, I say. What I got now is much better, much bigger. Sutter's involved, of course, and some others, but a sizable chunk is mine and as soon as I check in with Sutter's man on the location, I'll be off to Oregon to round up some worthy emigrants. It's the best spot on the bay, sunny out of the fog, right where the river comes in. It'll be the major port in a year mark my words. We're calling it San Francisca, pretty shrewd don't you think. How about a nice litte parcel right on the water?

No takers. Disgusted with them, Hastings pushed T. D. Jr. aside and rolled up his map. Buckdown asked Hastings if he knew Slant.

Yeah, I know him, Hastings said. He goes by the title of Money Balls. He's one of the worst land pirates on Battery Street. Don't buy anything from him. But don't worry, San Francisca will leave him sitting in the fog. You sure you're not interested in a nice sunny homesite?

Still no takers. Hastings climbed into his saddle and tipped his hat. Oh, by the way, he said, if you run into anybody named Donner, remember it wasn't my fault.

84/Battery Street

Ah yes, Battery Street, that thoroughfare of the shanghai and the rat fuck, that alley of manifest destiny, that Boardwalk of the dirty-minded monopoly game that brought Slant, Larkin, Brannan, Wild Emma, and a number of other equally civic-minded flimflammers and frontier capitalists together at Cargo West to talk business. Slant got directly to the point.

About this San Francisca, I don't know how far along it is, but it's sitting right next to the best deep-water anchorage in the whole bay. Not good. Then you take the name, San Francisca, pretty close to San Francisco, isn't it? Also not good. Figure that every dumbbell shipmaster, tourist, and settler headed in this direction says he's going to San Francisco. He means the bay, of course; the town he's heading for is Yerba Buena but he doesn't know that. You see the problem? If we don't do something, we could all lose a lot of business, not to mention what might happen to property values. Very bad indeed.

Everybody saw the problem and a notice appeared in the next edition of Brannan's paper.

AN ORDINANCE

Whereas, the local name of Yerba Buena, as applied to the settlement or town of San Francisco, is unknown beyond the district; and has been applied from the local name of the cove on which the town is built; *therefore*, to prevent confusion and fraud, and that the town may have the advantage of the name given on the public maps, it is hereby ordained that the name of San Francisco shall be *it* henceforth.

So be it and beware of facsimiles.

So Yerba Buena became San Francisco, and, after writing the ordinance, Slant went into seclusion. He took yet another room at Cargo West and converted it into an office. He took all meals alone in his expanded quarters and refused to answer the door, seeing only those he had one of the perfect Worm Eaters fetch for him. He was rumored to be scheming beyond the understanding of ordinary men. His power grew. Larkin didn't like it.

Larkin, you see, held property in San Francisca as well as in San Francisco. In fact, he held substantial property all over the territory, from Monterey to Los Angeles to various mountain lakes. He sent word to his partners that something would have to be done about the name. It had been chosen originally for two reasons. The first was obvious. The second was both shrewd and sentimental. Francisca happened to be the name of Vallejo's wife, so when Sutter had suggested to Larkin that they name the new town Francisco, he had said no, Francisca. Almost the same, but with the added possibility of an enhanced public image among the Californios who might yet have to be dealt with.

Larkin finished reading a letter from Mrs. Vallejo

and returned it to his portable files. It was her original plea for the release of her husband shortly after his capture by the Bear Flaggers. He looked at her signature. Francisca Benicia Felipsa Carrillo Vallejo. What a string of names! He closed his eyes and pointed. His finger fell on Benicia. He sent word to Sutter and moved on to the next problem.

What to do about Wild Emma? Was she still to be trusted? It was hard to say. Larkin blamed Pierre Wallingsford for the confusion. He had arrived in rags one day claiming to be a famous gambler and duelist from New Orleans. Then, somehow, he had slyly charmed his way into Wild Emma's bed and thus become part of the business. Now it looked like he was trying to take over. He had plans to introduce organized gambling at Cargo West and had also convinced Wild Emma to get rid of the Worm Eaters. Wallingsford would replace them, he said, with French whores from New Orleans who were already on the way. So instead of sending Richardson to pick up a fresh string of Worm Eaters from Hippolyte Weed, Wild Emma had been making do with the ones she had, in spite of numerous pregnancies, while she waited for the arrival of Wallingsford's French whores. The place was going to be much classier, she told Larkin.

Larkin wasn't sure. He thought she was getting a bit too ambitious and discussed the matter with the elegant Greek barman, who agreed totally. The barman had been in love with Wild Emma for some time and would agree with anything that might get rid of Wallingsford. They made a secret pact to eliminate him at the first opportunity, hopefully before Larkin had to return to Monterey. He wondered vaguely who Wallingsford was working for. Slant probably, but no one was above his suspicion, not even Vallejo.

TWENTY-ONE

85/Petaluma Adobe II

The freezing effect on wild animals of a bright light, or a snake paralyzing a mouse with a devouring stare, was much like the effect of Sewey's smile on his string of Worm Eaters. As he dragged them south, he amused himself by putting them through his own brutal kama sutra. It always started the same way. He lined them up, naked, and walked up and down the line frowning. When he smiled he had made a choice, and when he smiled at the unfortunate who was to be his pleasure, she froze, hypnotized by his dirty grin. By the time he had gone through the string three times, they were getting close to civilization. Sewey knew. He said he could smell it.

Sure enough, in the distance he saw the white walls of Vallejo's Petaluma Adobe. As he rode closer he could make out a crowd of mounted men milling around the front gate. The half-breed vaqueros were at play again, hooting and cheering from their saddles in another of their favorite pastimes. They were having a bull/bear dance, a recreation even more popular than a carrero del gallo.

A she-bear had been roped and dragged down from the hills. As Sewey rode up, several of the half-breeds were tying the other end of the rope to the horns of a lean red bull. Bets were made. The animals circled each other, stretching the rope between them. Suddenly, the bull charged. The bear lurched to one side and met the charge with a swipe that raked four shallow lines on the bull's flank. First blood. The half-breeds cheered. Sewey hustled his Worm Eaters inside the gate and hurried back to the action. He bet heavily on the bull.

Several more passes and the bull glistened with a shiny film of sweat, streaked with more lines of blood. The bull pawed the ground, reevaluating strategy. He began to circle the bear once again. The bear stood her ground, turning to face the next charge, waiting.

When it came the bear went for the bull's neck. With one paw she hooked into it like an anchor and grappled with the other for the nose. She tore at the bull's nose until he opened his mouth to let out a great roar and then she seized his tongue and pulled. The effect was remarkable. Sewey had never seen anything like it. The bull gentled, bleating pathetically, and the bear began pulling him about at will.

Dirty fighting, Sewey shouted.

The bear began spinning the bull about and finally

yanked the tongue with a slow whipping motion and the bull fell over on his back, the posture of submission known to all animals, a plea for mercy. The bear snorted. Still pulling mercilessly at the shredded tongue, she made two quick swipes with her other paw and the bull's head fell to one side, barely connected now to the thick neck. The half-breeds shot the bear and the dance was over.

Sewey had lost. Since he had no money to cover his bets, he was forced to make his Worm Eaters available to the half-breeds, and there ensued a long afternoon of payoff fornication in the bright courtyard of Vallejo's Petaluma Adobe.

Vallejo himself observed it from his balcony. He had returned to his former headquarters to rescue his library, planning to spend several days sorting things out. The bear bull dance had filled him with nostalgia. He determined to write a book about the old days. Now as he watched the stunt fucking beneath him in the courtyard, he was struck by a certain irony. Funny, he mused, how the Worm Eaters were probably the only ones who wouldn't lose anything to the Americans.

Sewey spotted Vallejo watching from the balcony and shouted up a question: Hey, you up there, you know any place that might be interested in some slightly used Worm Eaters?

Try Benicia.

86/The City of Francisca Benicia Felipsa Carrillo Vallejo

Turns out that Sutter's man at Benicia was Joaquin Peach. In one short month he had constructed a two-story wooden house for himself that also served as a real-estate office and hotel. So far, it was the town's only building, but it was full of fine furnishings. When Peach saw Taya, Buckdown, and T. D. Jr. staggering up to his front door, he laughed and started showing off.

The world turns, he said, grinning at Taya, and poked playfully at T. D. Jr.'s swollenness. He invited them into his large dining room, apologizing for the poor accommodations. He said he was sorry for his bad manners, his incompetence when it came to entertaining such esteemed guests. He pleaded with them to excuse his disgusting poverty, his wretched heritage, his weak bloodlines, his lack of formal education.

He mocked them until Taya could no longer stand it. She turned her back on him and his food and his linen sheets and rushed from the house. Buckdown and T. D. Jr. were too hungry to be proud. They fell gratefully on the food Peach laid out on the long table, while Taya walked alone on the flat beach. Peach watched her through the window. He liked her. The way she acted. He told Buckdown and T. D. Jr. to take whatever they wanted and headed for the · beach to apologize.

Taya had walked out on the point and stood staring out over the grey water. Peach came up behind her.

She did not turn around.

It is a fine world, he said. It will be fine for you and fine for your child.

She turned suddenly to face him. She bit her lip.

Children are for men, she said.

Yes, he said, and turned away.

Taya crossed the bay the next afternoon in Richardson's launch. It was a stroke of luck that the boatman had put in at Benicia. His backers had told him to stay clear of the place, but he was curious and wanted to take a short peek at the new city, maybe even pick up a little extra business. What Slant and the rest of them didn't know, Richardson figured, couldn't hurt him. So his Worm Eaters had rowed him past for a quick look and Peach had hailed him from the shore.

Buckdown sat in the stern listening to Richardson talk about the weather. T. D. Jr looked back toward the delta, haunted by the No See'ums. Taya pressed herself into the bow. She stared straight ahead, toward San Francisco emerging slowly before her, poking out of a dirty fog. The bay was flat and slick, smooth enough to scratch.

87/Sausalito

Shaboom and the Burgetts stood on the ridge high above Rancho Sausalito and looked out over the bay.

Galon was exhausted. Their trip down the coast from Fort Ross had been difficult. Millard was also a little beat, but Shaboom seemed charged with energy. He scurried back and forth on the ridge searching for the best view. Galon sat down on a flat rock and wondered where the Rancho Sausalito was.

It wasn't really a rancho at all, but a steepness of willow-and-brush-covered hillside that climbed up from a nicely sheltered little cove seven miles across the bay from Yerba Buena. Millard had heard of it. He explained that it was the home of a jack Catholic named Richardson, who had jumped an English whaler more than twenty years ago and obtained Californio status and the cove by marrying one of Vallejo's cousins. Richardson was known to be crafty, Millard said. His business was the ferrying of what-have-you about the bay by means of a launch in which he visited the various embarcaderos, making pickups and deliveries. He was also known to pirate pilot fees from any ship nosing into the bay. He called himself captain of the Port of San Francisco Bay and was active in many local schemes. He was also known to whoop it up several times a month at Cargo West.

Shaboom shouted for their attention and pointed toward Yerba Buena. A launch was pulling across the water in their direction. It had to be Richardson. Shaboom insisted that they take cover.

Peeking out from the brush on the ridge, Shaboom studied the launch. It was propelled by two rows of Worm Eaters who pulled rhythmically on long heavy oars. High in the stern sat a man in a dark blue cape. Occasionally he strung out a long whip to crack one of the Worm Eaters into a more enthusiastic approach to his oar. Shaboom shuddered and insisted that they make camp on the ridge, avoiding Richardson and his hovel below them on the lip of the cove.

They spent the next fortnight on the ridge while Shaboom studied the patterns of movement on the bay. Each morning, Worm Eaters in crude reed canoes could be seen poking tentatively out of the bay's tule fringes like water insects, and larger bargelike craft leap-frogged from cove to cove on the far shore, but only Richardson's launch crossed the bay with any regularity.

What they need here is a bridge, said Millard, who studied the bay at Shaboom's side.

TWENTY-TWO

88/Family Reunion

Taya followed Buckdown and T. D. Jr. into Cargo
West. Pierre Wallingsford was installing a gambling
wheel near the door. Small world. T. D. Jr. almost
bumped into him, but for some reason both acted as
if they had never before laid eyes on each other. Men
do that sometimes.

Wild Emma saw Taya and moved to her at once.
Pregnant women rattle the ambience of bars. Other
customers panic. Something always has to be done.
Rules must be set. Wild Emma ignored Buckdown
and T. D. Jr., and asked Taya if she was looking for
someone.

Before Taya could answer, Buckdown slapped his
hand down on the bar and tried to take charge.

That's right, he barked, where's Slant?

Oh, you mean Money Balls, Wild Emma said with a cagey smirk.

Slant, Buckdown boomed.

Old T. D. heard his name being batted about in the bar below and pressed an eye to one of his peepholes. His bifocal view of responsibility quickly distorted the scene below and caused him painful confusion. For a moment he thought Taya was her mother and T. D. Jr. was he. His peephole became a time scope, magnifying his guilt. But no, she wasn't her mother and his son was his son. Buckdown was the key, he looked so old. Old T. D. was relieved. He called one of the perfect Worm Eaters into his room and told him to fetch the family.

It was an awkward reunion. They had dinner sent up to the suite. Naturally, the one among them who had the least understanding of how they were all tied together did most of the talking. T. D. Jr. scattered bits and pieces of the last few months about the table like a chef pushing hors d'oeuvres at dinner guests whose hunger confused him.

Nobody ate much. They were sad, angry, and relieved, all four of them, all at once. Buckdown hated Slant for causing it all and then letting it happen. He felt bad about Taya, but he didn't know what to do for her. Slant hated Buckdown for causing it all and then letting it happen. He felt bad about Taya, but didn't know what to do for her. T. D. Jr. hated himself for not knowing what to do. He felt bad about Taya.

What are we going to do? T. D. Jr. wanted very much to know.

We take care of Taya, Buckdown said, and then we take care of them.

Like you did before, Slant sneered.

And you did?

Don't forget, Slant barked, I'm the one who lost his balls.

Obviously.

They were hopeless. Taya closed her eyes. They were hopeless and useless and didn't have the slightest fluttering notion of what was going on inside her. She felt like a glass jar full of expanding stones, transparent, about to crack open. When she opened her eyes again the three of them were staring at her. She hated them.

They could feel it.

89/T. D. Jr.

T. D. Jr. sharpened another pencil. Since the delta he had found it impossible to relax. His nerves bristled like quills. A twitch had developed deep in his chest. He tried to blame his condition on the No See'ums, but his problem was far too complicated to be the handiwork of invisible bugs and he knew it. He didn't know what he wanted to do. He wanted to speed the situation with Taya and Buckdown and his father toward resolution but couldn't decide where to begin. His father and Buckdown argued and plotted by themselves. Taya walked the beaches alone or brooded in her room. No one would talk to him. He felt left out.

In desperation he tried to work. Mornings, he scouted the various hills for appropriate angles from which to daguerreotype the bay but found that he couldn't concentrate. Most afternoons found him in Cargo West, shouting broken sentences at anyone, with the exception of Pierre Wallingsford, who happened to be at the bar. He got so rude that Wild Emma warned him to leave the other customers alone or risk being persona non grata at the bar. He quieted down but began drinking heavily to show her who was boss. He slashed hysterical line drawings into his sketchbooks, breaking pencils, waiting for resolve.

90/Fatherhood

Slant and Buckdown never settled the question of who Taya's father was. It was impossible to tell. She looked a little like both of them. Her skin was very clear, deep, and smooth like Buckdown's. Her hands were slender, almost elegant, like Slant's. But in looking vaguely like both of them, she looked like neither of them. They both thought she looked like her mother. High cheekbones, larger eyes perhaps, but the same rich, black hair and full, round mouth. And now that she was nine-months pregnant, she seemed so soft and rounded and yet so very slender, like her mother had looked carrying her. But she had no father.

Both Buckdown and Slant were sure it was the other guy. They each figured that if she were his daughter, he would know it. Just know it somehow, and neither did. But they didn't want to know. It was more comfortable for them both that way. It was perhaps the only way that either man could make his separate peace with the memory of her mother.

91/Joaquin Peach

When it came to questions of fatherhood, it turned out that Joaquin Peach had more character than Slant and Buckdown combined. When he was told that his favorite little Worm Eater at Cargo West was pregnant, he naturally assumed that she was carrying his child. And instead of ignoring her, he surprised everyone by stomping into Cargo West and buying her from Wild Emma. The men at the bar thought it was a big joke, but Peach was serious. He took her shopping and then had Richardson ferry them back to his new house at Benicia. It had nothing to do with love, Peach told himself, although he would surely love his son. It was a matter of birthrights.

When they stepped ashore at Benicia he told her that he would name the child after Pizarro. She smiled. She had no idea who Pizarro was but was very happy to get away from Cargo West. She determined to make Peach happy. Perhaps some day she would tell him about the strange Mormon. His visits had been her only pleasure at Cargo West, even if she was not sure of the meaning of the strange eye that stared at her through the ceiling whenever the Mormon had come to call.

Much to Peach's surprise, he found her mysterious and interesting and pleasant to have around. She cooked for him and mended his clothes and was careful to clean things up or make things messy as he preferred. Christmas was coming and she seemed to add the appropriate warmth to his house, even though she was a pagan. He said that she was perfect for now, that he had started his line with her and that was all that mattered.

92 / Zorro

Although it is not clear when and where Zorro and His Own Ghost got together, they must have. How else to explain Zorro's new style? When Taya came upon the old folk hero on the western slope of Telegraph Hill, he was on his hands and knees, helping field rodents repair some collapsed burrows; and gone were his swashbuckling black silks, replaced by bits of foliage and animal parts of the sort favored by His Own Ghost.

You've changed, Taya said.

So have you, Zorro told her. Which one did you wind up marrying?

No marriages.

Then you'd better marry me, Zorro said.

It was outrageous, to be sure, but then up until now no one had bothered to ask her. She wasn't about to marry anybody. That's not the kind of a girl she was. But it was, finally, rather nice to be asked.

That's nice, Taya said, but no.

Why not? I live with the animals now. You'd like it.

Taya explained that it would be better if they were just real good friends. And, as seldom happens, from that point on they were.

TWENTY-THREE

93/Christmas Cheer

The Christmas celebration at Cargo West lasted three days. It was a mass drunk. Wild Emma hung pine boughs from the ceiling and the smell of fresh pitch mixed pleasantly with the stink of brandy and tobacco smoke. At one point a food fight erupted and chunks of smoked goose, bits of anchovy sauce, and bread pudding flew across the room and spattered the walls. Buckdown got drunk for the first time in sixteen years and tried to deliver a sermon relating to the spiritual life of animals. He was hooted down. The pilot contingent of Pierre Wallingsford's French whores had finally arrived from New Orleans and wound up giving it away. T. D. Jr. slumped in a corner, his head lolling, and blithered odd bits of esthetic theory at the customers. Even old Money Balls joined the festivities.

In the end, the celebrants heaped together in a tangle on the floor and commenced to amuse themselves in a most unearthly howling. According to eyewitness accounts, some growled like dogs while others roared like bulls. A few hissed like snakes. But most had crossed into a state of debauchery where they could imitate nothing save their own animalized selves. Taya was not amused.

She resented their fun, their celebration of their own blind humanity. The child was very close now. She felt it kicking out the cadence of a wasted life, her life, aged and gone joyless, made hopeless by the unwanted little shit she carried inside her. She walked along the bay, watching the water birds, aching to fly out of herself, to get away. She felt the closeness of life like a heavy suffocating blanket. Hers was a bitter and finite despair with the cycle of life itself.

In the dunes, she would lie on her back and scoop the cold sand up over herself in a mock burial. Then, tightening her body like a coil, she felt the vibrations of the two hearts beating inside her and screamed in angry bursts until her throat ached.

Noel! Noel!

94/A Strange Worm Eater

Shaboom scanned the bay. Two gunships with stars and stripes drooping over their taffrails lay side by side off San Francisco. He could see men in striped jerseys moving about their decks like blue and white

ants. Three seagoing merchant vessels of question-
able registry creaked in the tide closer to the mud
flats. They were visited constantly by an array of rafts
and cargo skiffs. The same old view.

Shaboom moved to a spot on the ridge where he
could see the mouth of the bay. His heart jumped.
Finally, it was the *Eagle*. He shouted to the Burgetts.
They watched the handsome vessel run smoothly
into the bay, her sails snapping in the crosswinds.
Shaboom pointed with glee to raking masts, obviously set for speed, her brass capstan heads and
bells glinting in the sun, her mahogany rails sturdy
and elegant. He jumped up and down with anticipation. It was time to move.

He decided that Millard could handle Richardson
and whoever had to be dealt with once they crossed
the bay. He would go along, of course, but disguised
as Millard's Worm Eater, to avoid close scrutiny.
Galon was in no condition to move unless it was
absolutely necessary, so he would stay with the gold.
Shaboom explained his plan, then took off all his
clothes and rolled in the dirt. He then threw a crusty
deerskin over his head and told Millard to lead him
to Richardson's dock.

It worked. Richardson fell for the disguise so completely that he insisted Shaboom help out his own
Worm Eaters with the pull across the bay. Shaboom
blistered his hands on one of the starboard oars,
while Richardson talked about the weather and ad-
vised Millard that he could find whatever he was
looking for at Cargo West.

The purchase of passage for three to the Orient on
the *Eagle*, to sail in ten days, was accomplished with-

out incident that afternoon by Millard, who slyly booked himself round trip. He made the arrangements over brandy at Larkin's table at Cargo West with few questions asked. Larkin thought Millard's name was familiar but he couldn't place it. Old T. D. Slant could have refreshed his memory, of course, had he not been arguing with Buckdown on the floor above.

Since business was light at that time of day, Millard's Worm Eater was allowed to accompany his master in the bar, as long as he squatted unobtrusively under the table, which suited Shaboom perfectly. He could hear everything without being noticed, or so he thought until he peeked out between Millard's knees and saw a nervous young man studying him from the bar.

It was T. D. Jr., passing yet another day with his sketch pad, anticipating the arrival of the supplies he had ordered through Larkin and brooding over Taya's refusal to let him comfort her. It is hard to say what he would have done had he known the identity of the man he saw dealing with Larkin. As it was, T. D. Jr. ignored him and concentrated on the peculiar figure under the table, fascinated by the flat round face with the slit eyes. Not your average Worm Eater, in spite of the familiar posture. T. D. Jr. sketched him emerging from a dark background as if from a cave.

Shaboom was unnerved by T. D. Jr.'s focused attention and yanked at Millard's pants legs. Millard understood and stood up, dropping several gold nuggets in front of Larkin as a deposit.

Where'd you get these?

Working for Sutter, Millard told him.

But before Larkin could make further inquiries, Millard had led Shaboom out the door to find Richardson.

Their passage back to Sausalito was choppy but uneventful. Shaboom pulled at his oar among the silent Worm Eaters and popped all the blisters he had developed that morning. Yet he barely felt the pain, preoccupied as he was by the possible motives of that crazy young man at the bar.

Millard meanwhile sat confidently in the bow, pleased that all had gone well. He figured that everything had been taken care of without raising suspicion, and he reflected upon his new intelligence. He enjoyed being smarter than he had been before; too bad he wasn't quite as smart as he thought he was.

Larkin was naturally suspicious as hell. As soon as he had examined the nuggets, he sent one of the perfect Worm Eaters to fetch Joaquin Peach. When Peach came to him the next day, Larkin dispatched him to Sutter with a message on a piece of cloth wrapped around one of the larger nuggets like a fist.

The message was to come at once.

95/Sewey

There are some men who circle the edges of civilization like scavengers, men who by their existence alone spew the anguish of everyday survival over the collective consciousness of everybody else. They view life as a dirty joke and lurk the frontiers delivering punch lines of rancid sex and violence. Josiah Sewey, as we have already seen, was such a man, and at Benicia his psychopathy erupted once again.

He arrived late in the afternoon. A pregnant Worm Eater was sitting in front of the house mending a pair of Joaquin Peach's billowing white pants. Sewey could hear her humming on the cool breeze coming in off the water. He had not used any of his Worm Eaters since he had paid off the half-breeds with them at Vallejo's Petaluma Adobe. They had seemed dirty and boring to him since then. The Worm Eater he saw before him in the late afternoon sun, however, was different. She looked good to him. He pushed his Worm Eaters up to the house and inquired about something to eat.

She nodded and pointed to the string. She knew where they were headed. She had arrived at Cargo West the same way. How long ago she wasn't sure. Could she give them something to eat, too?

Sewey didn't answer. While she went ahead and prepared some food, he prowled silently through the house. He found no signs of her master, no guns, and decided she was alone. He returned to the porch and waited for her to serve him.

After he had eaten, she asked for payment. He laughed and unbuttoned his pants. She hit him in the shoulder with the pot she had served him from and ran into the house. He cursed and followed her, rubbing his shoulder.

Time passed in brutal slapstick. He chased her about the kitchen. She hurled pots and cups at him. He swatted them away and grabbed at her clothes. She turned furniture over in front of him. He slapped her face. She screamed for help. His Worm Eaters watched from the doorway. She yelled that if they would help her kill him they would be free. He shouted that he would kill them all.

He caught her by the hand and smashed at her face. She dropped to the floor and he fell heavily on top of her. The suddenly his Worm Eaters, still tied together, came up behind him and began beating on his back. She came to beneath him and clawed at his eyes.

He exploded in rage. With a roaring heave, he threw them from his back and leaped to his feet, stomping down over and over with his heavy boot. Her face split open like a melon. He spit and turned to his Worm Eaters. They were crying hysterically, trying to run. He caught their rope and yanked. They fell and he dragged them screaming outside.

He beat them and then staked them spread-eagle on the ground. He wanted to fuck them all but his limp cock would not rise. He ranted that they were to blame and fucked them with his rifle. He rammed the cold barrel into them one after another until they began to pass out, and then he climaxed into each with a squeeze of the trigger.

When he was finished, the moon had risen. He felt better. He looked down and saw his cock finally rising erect in the silver light.

96/Taya

Across the bay Taya prepared herself for the birth of the child by thinking about death. Buckdown had suggested it, telling her to smile at the inevitable and try to see the circles in the sky. Turn, turn, turn, and all that. Seasons, rebirth, dogs fighting and fucking in the night streets under her window. She saw the crescent moon, a lunatic death-smile pinned to a black sky hanging over the bay like a tarp.

Moon, she said, it is not fair.

Of course not, said the moon, grinning at her.

TWENTY-FOUR

97/The Hounds

The new year cracked open like a broken mirror. Another celebration had taken place at Cargo West and even lower-minded debauches occurred at less prestigious establishments. The entire population of San Francisco wandered irritably through the muddy streets, bumping and jostling into each other as if gone sightless in their communal hangover. Tempers flashed. Duels and vendettas, muggings and more obvious assaults mixed in a frenzy of general bad manners. Heroes, if there had ever been any, went into hiding and the Hounds were born.

A fraternity of sorts, the Hounds organized with the declared purpose of assisting each other in sickness or when shortage or peril threatened any of their number. The result, of course, was a gang of public robbers. They affected uniforms, principally a sleeveless canvas jacket or vest with copulating dogs crudely sketched on the back, and pretended to be governed by a kind of military discipline. On the first Sunday of the new year, they paraded the streets in the name of law and order, and then spent the following day in the tents of inoffensive newcomers, extorting whatever the unfortunates had of value.

Word of the Hounds spread fast, coming to Sewey as he rounded the southern tip of the bay. It was interesting news. After he settled with Wild Emma he might just join up. He smiled at the future, the options.

Brannan, meanwhile, was worried as hell. The Hounds, he told Slant, could turn into a serious threat to law and order. And worse, suppose they were secretly working for Sutter, instigated by him to give San Francisco a bad name, while Benicia beckoned to newcomers like a peaceful nest from across the bay. The value of real estate could drop, Brannan cried, his real estate.

Slant told him to relax. Any publicity was good publicity, he said. He had other things on his mind.

He felt terrible about his family, such as it was. Taya was brooding and hostile toward him. She rejected his every gesture of compassion. Guilt gnawed at him. Then there was his own son, obviously on the verge of nervous collapse. The lad seemed to be drifting, tied to some mad organ grinder who couldn't get the rhythms straight; and he, too, his own flesh and blood, seemed to despise him, blame him.

Then there was Buckdown, goading him constantly through some maze of mutual guilt and responsibility. Old bones kept coming up between them, pushing them into corners they had both seen before. They kicked through the purple winter flowers on the hill behind Cargo West, arguing over how to go about things, what things to go about first, and *what things were about*. They appalled each other.

The book was your idea, Buckdown grumbled.

Yeah, Slant hissed, but it was your idea to share.

98/His Own Ghost

The old shaman was drawn to Benicia as if by a magnet. It was his job, after all, to make sure that the ghosts of the dead Worm Eaters made the correct choice. What form to take on the journey to the Dead Place was a serious matter. One did not want to get caught in the Sacred Time as a puma when one really needed to be a silver trout, for example.

So His Own Ghost looked at the mutilated young Worm Eaters, considered them with his heart, and tried to be helpful. He ate a mouthful from his medicine pouch and sat down among the corpses. Soon he had a song:

> *I dream*
> *I dream of you*
> *I dream of you flying.*

That was all he had to sing.

99/Sewey

One thing that Sewey knew was that you didn't just ride into a new town alone. Nope, you scoped it first, preferably from an elevated point of vantage, a hill. He was certainly right about that, a man with as many enemies as himself had to take certain precautions. Too bad for him that he picked the very hill where Zorro lived, the hill where the old folk hero and Taya were passing another morning as real good friends. And especially too bad for Sewey that His Own Ghost would also be making the scene momentarily.

Congratulating himself on his canny moves, Sewey tied his horse out of sight in a cluster of oak and started making his way carefully up the slope. Close to the top he looked off to his left, and there, in a notch just below the summit, he spotted Taya and Zorro. And thinking them just a couple of easy pickings, he headed over to see what he could get off them. He was just about close enough to recognize Taya, when he got whacked unconscious by a blow from his own saddle gun wielded by His Own Ghost, who also happened to be riding Sewey's own horse.

Sewey went down in a spread, arms and legs flung out, his back to the dirt. Taya stared at him. A chill, then a flutter, raced around her brain and she decided not to smash Sewey's skull with any of the handy rocks. It would be much better, she suddenly knew, to stake him down naked there on top of Telegraph Hill and walk away.

This is the best way, she said to Zorro and His Own Ghost. I have a feeling.

His Own Ghost smiled and scanned the sky.

100/Condors

The few citizens of what was now San Francisco who noticed the huge birds circling Telegraph Hill wondered what was up. Such giants usually glided clear of the tricky thermals and squalls that dominated the region. All of the local Worm Eaters naturally understood right off that the Animal People were around.

The birds circled all day, finally settling at dusk. The night that followed was moonless and especially cold, driving all but the Worm Eaters to early sleep. And in that sleep not one of them heard the shrieks that shot like electric currents blowing downwind off the hill. But the Worm Eaters heard and stayed alert through the night, smiling with each whistling cry.

And at dawn, only the Worm Eaters saw the huge birds rising in hard arcs, then swooping into an elegant ballet high out over the bay.

TWENTY-FIVE

101/Taya

A pack of large dogs waited open-mouthed on the mud flats, anxious to bark. Shaboom and the Burgetts slid across the water in Richardson's launch. Only Millard took notice of the mangle of bones that dropped out of the sky and splashed with a rattle off their stern in the middle of the bay.

Ahead of them in San Francisco, Cargo West was packed. Sutter and Joaquin Peach had arrived, having come straight through by small boat without stopping at Benecia. They sat with Larkin, whispering back and forth. At the next table Brannan made a list of potential members for a vigilance committee he planned to organize against the Hounds.

Pierre Wallingsford tinkered with his gambling wheel. Slant and Buckdown argued at their regular table. T. D. Jr. stood at the bar, slashing into his sketchbook. It was midmorning of a day that hung naked off the trunk of the new year like a branch of overripe fruit. Outside, the *Eagle* was preparing to sail, and upstairs, Taya was going into labor.

She pressed deeper into old T. D.'s feather mattress and waited for the next pain. She began counting each breath. The windowless room was cool and dark. There was a knock at the door.

Go away, Taya said.

Wild Emma opened the door and walked in with a pan of warm water and a stack of towels. She set them on the table and sat down next to Taya on the bed.

No sweat, she said, it's a very natural thing. She started dabbing a white handkerchief at Taya's forehead. Taya slapped her hand away.

Get out.

Wild Emma rose stiffly from the bed, smoothing her skirt. Little whore, she muttered, and walked out of the room.

Taya closed her eyes and kept counting. An image of Sewey and the Burgetts learing over her barged into her mind. She stiffened. Another pain. It was the same thing all over again, inside out this time but the same. She began to thrash about on the bed. Suddenly she couldn't move. Someone was holding her arms. She opened her eyes and saw His Own Ghost. The shaman must have snuck up the back stairs. He smiled at her and released his grip. Taya relaxed.

His Own Ghost began to strip. He hung bits of fur and animal teeth about the room. He placed soft translucent pouches in the corners and under the table. He draped his bone-and-feather cape over the bed. He plucked twigs and sprouts from his mucky crotch and planted them in cracks in the wooden walls. Soon he began to mumble and hum, sliding about the room without lifting his feet. The lizard heads wobbled rhythmically to and fro. A soft, almost golden light seemed to glow from his pink eyes. He grew paler.

When Taya closed her eyes again Sewey and the Burgetts were gone. She concentrated on the pains. They were coming faster now. She didn't care. She began to push.

102/Come Together

Clatter shouts and shit screams pumped like a fountain when Shaboom and the two Burgetts walked into Cargo West. Showers of accusation, terror, recognition; low-breed reason went mad.

It's them!

Suddenly, the flash of weapons, but Larkin was way ahead of everyone as usual. He had signaled the elegant Greek barman who pulled a shotgun from beneath the bar and froze the room. Now . . . Larkin stood on a chair.

One step at a time, he said.

Bastards, Slant screamed. Justice!

Shut up, Sutter shouted. That's the least of our problems.

Gold, Brannan said. Look at it all.

In the confusion, Galon Burgett had dropped his

traveling bag, and gold nuggets had spilled over the floor at his feet.

Where'd you get the gold? Larkin demanded.

Millard explained, said there was lots of it, plenty to go around.

Yeah, Galon wheezed, you guys get your own.

We can't let this get out, Sutter began to plead, tears forming in his eyes. It's too early. I'm not ready.

Good point, said Brannan.

Perhaps, said Larkin.

Fuck the gold, said Buckdown.

I want their balls, Slant screamed.

Larkin raised his hands for silence, but suddenly another surprise: Zorro slid through the door, obviously with a lesson to teach. He reached behind his back and produced Sewey's little purse. He tossed it, and Slant watched his scrotum turn slowly in the air and land with a heavy plop on the dark mahogany bar.

Upstairs, His Own Ghost splashed the child in the pan of warm water, and Taya opened her eyes. Voices again, wafting up to her through old T. D.'s peepholes. She heard him and Buckdown, then Larkin and Wild Emma and, finally, Sutter arguing, pleading that the most important consideration for all of them is keeping the lid on. Silence for a moment and then she heard another voice; less familiar, but one she would never forget. Galon Burgett.

What's in it for me? he was saying.

Taya was quickly out of bed and on her hands and knees, staring through the largest peephole. Beneath her, old T. D., Buckdown, and the rest were standing in a half-circle around Shaboom and the Burgetts. Guns and knives lay in a pile between them. Larkin was now sitting on the bar, flanked by the elegant barman and Wild Emma and their shotguns. A deal was going down but Taya didn't hear. She reached under the bed for her saddle gun and old T. D.'s double-barreled pistol. She checked the loads and poked all three barrels through the floor at Galon. A tight fit and difficult to aim, but she managed. She held her breath and pulled all three triggers at once.

Blam! Gunfire sprayed down on the barroom. Most dove for cover, some went for weapons. Wild Emma and the Greek both fired. Galon went down, Millard went out the window. Buckdown rolled across the floor with his pistol pumping one, two, three holes into Galon's already dead body.

Taya grabbed the bedpost and pulled herself to her feet, headed for the back stairs.

In the bar, Larkin called things back to order. Galon was definitely dead: natural causes, according to old T. D. Also dead was Pierre Wallingsford, his face splattered with buckshot, probably hit by the elegrant Greek barman. T. D. Jr. was bleeding slightly from the shoulder; Wild Emma's shot most likely. Slant and Brannan were gulping brandy. Buckdown was reloading and peeking out the window after Millard.

Sutter crawled out from under the table where he'd taken shelter with that strange Worm Eater. Now, he, said, about keeping the lid on.

Outside, the first thing Taya noticed was the bay, the blueness of it set off against the thick white fog

tumbling in its afternoon roll through the headlands.
She smiled. Whitecaps were blowing across the
water like feathers. She began to hum, and by the
time she reached the dunes she was singing.

103/Millard

Millard went with the flow, so to speak. Actually, he
hit the bay at a dead run at the foot of Battery Street,
and then dogpaddled with the current until he
caught the rising tide which hooked him north and
then west, finally flopping him ashore in the dunes
around the point.

He lay face down in the sand, fleas crawling in and
out of his ears. Boy, did he have some thinking to
do. But time had already begun to slip away from
him. First he heard a sound so soft he thought it was
coming off the bay on the fog. But no, it was someone humming, singing actually. He lifted his head
and opened his eyes straight into the twin barrels of
a pistol that had fired on him not an hour before.
Tears welled in his eyes and he began to smile, the
vacant optimistic smile that he had forgotten was
part of him.

You'd be right to shoot, he said.

And she did.

104/The Code of the West

When Taya returned from the beach, Larkin had everything settled. A cover-up had been worked out and everyone at Cargo West had signed a secret agreement. They stood around drinking, congratulating themselves. It was assumed that Millard had drowned.

Taya watched them for a moment through the window, then made her way up the back stairs. She fell facedown on the bed and was asleep at once. His Own Ghost had disappeared. And so had the child.

TWENTY-SIX

105/Accidental Lives

Strange how lives can turn so completely in one short year, and how most of them keep turning. The accidental life, Slant called it, although it was certainly no accident that the discovery of gold was postponed for close to a year.

And what a year it was, very busy for most, sad and brutal for some. The Walla Walla Irregulars returned to Sutter's Fort complaining that the looting had been scattered at best. Sutter tried to pacify them with whisky and a few more horses, but Yellow Serpent was very bitter, and on their return to Oregon the Walla Walla behaved very badly.

When Joaquin Peach returned to Benicia and found the carnage left by Sewey, his mind went winging off into such a private despair that perhaps only Buckdown might have understood. The roto quit Sutter and isolated himself high in the Sierra. When the gold rush broke he took up the life of a wild bandit, using his mother's maiden name, Murietta. He became a great hero among the poor and was immortalized after his death in romantic literature.

Almost everybody else tried to get rich quick. Some did, some didn't. Larkin, of course, was wealthy already and his fortunes continued to increase. That strange Worm Eater, Shaboom, was allowed to keep the passages booked by Millard on the *Eagle*. When he reached Hong Kong he sold the remaining tickets to two Chinamen and one Chinawoman, and reached Yedo with some cash in his pocket. Wild Emma married the elegant Greek barman and together they prospered, controlling at one point more than one hundred operations patterned after Cargo West.

Vallejo hung on to what he could and lived to author a five-volume history of California that remains obscure and unread to this day. Sutter, in spite of his elaborate plotting, fared worse. He was overrun by hordes of argonauts and lost most of his vast holdings, in spite of numerous petitions to the government. Most legislators and bureaucrats found his babbling about divine right laughable, and he died broken and ignored in Washington, D. C.

Slant would have loved it had he not been long gone himself by then. While others scrambled for leverage in the tense months before the discovery was announced, Slant patched together a lurid and sensational exposé of Mormon sexual habits. He and Buckdown then used it to extort a substantial sum from Brannan before they traveled together to the most remote of the Sandwich Islands. They were never heard from again, although it was rumored that Slant had murdered Buckdown shortly after their arrival and bribed the natives to make it look like a surfing accident.

Brannan was an easy mark for men like Slant and many of them found him. He made several fortunes but lost them all just as quickly. He died drunk and penniless in Mexico in 1889.

T. D. Jr. remained in San Francisco for sixty years. He achieved minor fame during the gold rush for his stark portraits of luckless miners but did not keep up with the scientific development of his craft and wound up living quietly on an inheritance from his mother. He died from a heart attack in the early moments of the famous earthquake of 1906. His landlady claimed that he ran into the street screaming that it was about time and dropped dead.

106/Taya

Taya kept moving. Some said she had murdered her own child, but she didn't care. Just kept moving. Going to the beach a lot. Like a real Californian.